# THERE'S A
# MONSTER
# BEHIND
# THE DOOR

# THERE'S A MONSTER BEHIND THE DOOR

## GAËLLE BÉLEM

*Translated by*
**KAREN FLEETWOOD**
**&**
**LAËTITIA SAINT-LOUBERT**

bullaun press

First published 2024 by
**BULLAUN PRESS**
Sligo, Ireland
www.bullaunpress.com

10 9 8 7 6 5 4 3 2 1

Originally published in French as *Un monstre est là, derrière la porte*
Copyright © Éditions Gallimard, Paris, 2020

Translation copyright © Karen Fleetwood, Laëtitia Saint-Loubert, 2024
Text copyright © Gaëlle Bélem, 2020, 2024

Paperback ISBN 978 1 7398423 6 9
Ebook ISBN 978 1 7398423 7 6

Bullaun Press gratefully acknowledges the financial support of the Arts Council / An Chomhairle Ealaíon.

This book was published with the support of Literature Ireland.

Cet ouvrage a bénéficié du soutien du Programme d'aide à la publication de l'Institut français.

Printed in Spain by Castuera

Set in 11pt on 16pt Adobe Garamond Pro by Niall McCormack

'That's the way it is and that's that.'

Such is the unwavering response that the nameless narrator from *There's a Monster Behind the Door* keeps getting from her parents, the Dessaintes, every time she tries to make sense of the nonsensical world around her. What world is that? La Réunion, in the 1980s, described by the author as 'a heap of rubble on the edge of the world'. Had the narrator had more caring parents, she might have been told that La Réunion is located in the South West Indian Ocean, and that together with Mauritius and Rodrigues, it constitutes the Mascarene Islands. It is also a French overseas territory known as a *Département et Région d'Outre-Mer* (*DROM*), together with Martinique, Guadeloupe, Guyane (French Guiana) and Mayotte. But this is the Dessaintes household you are about to enter, so beware: information is sparse, language can be forceful, and cultural references are monstrous! Welcome to the Dessaintes' world!

*There's a Monster Behind the Door* is Gaëlle Bélem's first novel. It is also the first novel by a Reunionese woman writer to be published by French publishing giant Gallimard in their *Continents noirs* series. In the wake of the Black Lives Matter movement, the English translation of this novel seemed a timely and urgent enterprise. All the more so as Reunionese literature remains fairly unknown in the Anglophone world. Our translation therefore aims to introduce the English-speaking reader to a literature that deserves to be seen and heard.

Reunionese literature often destabilizes the French language through its strong oral, Creole component, known as *kréol rényoné*. Gaëlle Bélem's novel is no exception to this tradition. The author peppers her text with snippets of *kréol rényoné*, at times explicit, at others more latent, while renegotiating French through linguistic and syntactical deviation. As translators, we felt it was crucial to retain a similar sense of variation in the English version, so we kept and brought to the surface of the text Creole and French expressions to immerse the English-speaking reader in La Réunion. We included immediate gloss in the translation and reproduced some of the author's original notes only where necessary. We further felt it was essential to reflect the original work's linguistic diversity in the target language and opted for a translation that similarly echoes various English*es*.

For the French reader unfamiliar with La Réunion, references to the island's history, its rich cultural, sociolinguistic, religious and ethnographic mixed heritage, as well as its unique Creole culinary traditions, may feel unsettling at first. We wanted to preserve similar reading conditions for the English-speaking reader. For example, we kept words such as *Z'arabes, Zoreils, Malabars, Yabs* and *Cafres*, along with their derivatives, in the translation, as those terms are commonly used on the island to refer to its mixed population, composed, respectively, of Muslims, White metropolitan French people, Indians, poor Whites, and people of African and Malagasy descent. The term *Cafre* (*Kaf* in *kréol rényoné*) is derived from the Arab word *kafir*, meaning 'infidel'. In South Africa, using the 'K-word' is now condemned as hate speech. In La Réunion, *Cafre/Kaf* is not used as an ethnic slur and can be found in expressions like the annual 'Fet Kaf', which commemorates the abolition of slavery on the island on 20 December 1848.

Rendering the culture and humour present in the original French was one of the main challenges we faced while translating *There's a Monster Behind the Door*. We decided to keep the original flavour of traditional Creole dishes like *carri* (Reunionese curry) and *rougail* (spicy sauce or stew) in the translation to preserve the specificities of Reunionese cuisine in the English language. Similarly, whenever a Reunionese word, expression or image was used in the original French, we aimed to keep it in the translation to make English-speaking readers aware of the diglossic realities of La Réunion and of the power differentials at work between so-called 'major' and 'minor' languages. Puns, play-on-word jokes and a general sense of wry humour present throughout Gaëlle Bélem's novel constituted another challenge. We felt we needed to adapt some of these features for an Anglophone audience, while preserving the original's essence.

The collaborative nature of our project certainly presented challenges of its own, but above all it provided us with a unique space for mutual reflection, creation and negotiation, whereby both the original and the target language were constantly reappraised and redirected, echoing the creolization at work in Gaëlle Bélem's sublime first novel. We hope that the reader will feel both at home in and yet unhomed by this reading experience. And that Reunionese literature gets the place it deserves in the global literary scene through more translations. We warmly thank Bridget Farrell from Bullaun Press for allowing this project to come to light. 'And that's that.'

Karen Fleetwood and Laëtitia Saint-Loubert

To
Pascal F.
Claire K.
Anne H.

M.G.A

'I would not dwell where tempests never come
for they bring beauty in their train.'

THOMAS COLE

'That's the way it is and that's that!'

While parents usually get carried away trying to explain the great mysteries of life and the why and wherefore of everything to their offspring, the Dessaintes always proved exceptionally mean when it came to explanations.

Of course, they attached a degree of importance to feeding and clothing the only child they had brought into the world, and to making her generally presentable, but never – not once – did they show any zeal for instruction, let alone education.

Their attachment to the most basic platitudes and their innate laziness when it came to answering their child's questions was perhaps a symptom of their resignation, of their submissive acceptance of realities beyond their understanding, of their total lack of education. Whatever the reason, they dismissed all her inquiries – those questions from a child mesmerized by the world – with the same laconic, fixed response: 'That's the way it is and that's that!'

Farewell science and its complicated algorithms, farewell erudite digressions and their gang of bearded boffins! In the small town of Saint-Benoît, or to be more precise at number 21 rue René-Descartes (which they naturally misspelled as 'René des Cartes'), the mere sight of a book was enough to make the Dessaintes' hair stand on end, sending them into a state of acute irritation followed by inescapable ennui.

Welcome to the island of La Réunion in the 1980s: a heap of rubble on the edge of the world where the worst human superstitions, chased out by waves of European scepticism, had finally found a welcoming harbour. Here they had been able to take root and grow, and now cast a terrible shadow over a headstrong and utterly gullible people.

During the day, the streets were indolent rows of houses flanked by letterboxes full of bills and other official correspondence, but come night-time, it was a tropical Halloween over and over. Every neighbourhood was given over to a legion of invisible tyrants: Néréides, Nazgûl and other misanthropic, carnivorous and barbarous demons who were held accountable for all the mishaps and mistakes of the day. At least, that's what my parents, the parents of my parents, the parents of the parents of my parents, their own great-grandparents, their friends, the friends of their enemies and the enemies of their friends swore – and the conversation ended there. Or rather, it persisted there, growing and spreading like wildfire across the island's twenty-four municipalities, its three *cirques*,[1] its savannah and its two

---

1 Topographical depression in the shape of a circle or semicircle surrounded by steep cliffs. La Réunion has three such cirques, literally speaking, namely Salazie, Mafate and Cilaos, to which a more figurative 'cirque' that of the Dessaintes, can be added. [Translators' note: *cirque* in French also means circus.]

2

volcanoes, until there was not a single resident left, with the exception of the *Zoreils*,[2] who doubted the existence of the devil, his wanton wickedness and his control over pretty much anything and everything.

The very youngest knew not to ask too many questions, for bloodthirsty monsters were always eavesdropping at doors and, come nightfall, would like nothing more than to gobble up a nosey child!

If the Dessaintes' child nevertheless insisted on knowing the reason for which something was forbidden, the why of the breeze that blew, the how of the Mascarene martin[3] that sang, or the wherefore of a rainbow's formation – and if they were cornered into providing an explanation slightly longer than the usual eight words – the Dessaintes immediately blurted out the most frightful stories, an avalanche of unpredictable, vivid and irrefutable horrors. This all to smother the child's curiosity, to prevent her from any new investigation and to stunt her desire to listen and to talk. This may have been all well and good. Except for the fact that this child, their only child, was me!

In short, my parents, to whom fate had given the name Dessaintes, were horrible Creole versions of the monosyllabic Bartleby coupled with that nutcase Lovecraft – not that they'd ever know enough to recognize that about themselves! They were driven by a single abject certainty: the best way to bring up children was to

---

2    Term used in La Réunion to designate a white person from mainland France.

3    Small black bird from under whose tongue a muscle is cut to make it capable of repeating numerous words, much to the dismay of those who protect wildlife.

shut them up by terrorizing them! Rather than explain things, they petrified them, and they never resorted to persuasion because it was easier to intimidate.

For example: after a long, lively dinner one evening, I decided to hoist myself up on a chair and climb onto the table. Just like that, without any reason. Normal parents would have immediately held out their arms to coax their naughty tot back down. With a disapproving look, they would have explained that, through such behaviour, the child was exposing itself to danger – they may break their bones were they to fall. But the Dessaintes were not normal. My dad finished picking his teeth, poured himself another glass of water and, his eyes still fixated on the television, simply asked me:

'Do you know what happens to children who climb on tables?'

And without even waiting for my reply, he continued, 'They are condemned to live their entire lives as dwarves. Spotty and full of pus. Just like Tom the Troll. Remember him? Our neighbour with the club foot and the harelip? Found dead last year, devoured by ants and swarming with maggots? If Tom had listened to his parents, who knows the life he'd have led! He wasn't born like that. He became like that. And you will too. After just a minute on the table, the curse can't be reversed, you know! That's the way it is and that's that!'

Then, with enormous gravity, my father began looking at his watch.

I was immediately consumed by fear. A gnawing, harrowing terror filled my body as I searched my father's face for some sign that he was joking. None came. Tom, Tom the Troll, that gnome from Saint-Benoît, feared by all the children of rue Descartes – even Big Johnny who wasn't afraid of anything, not even his mother! Tom the Gnome, whose only friend was a dog. We all wondered which of them had given the other mange. If he were still alive, at least we could have been friends, I thought. I was terror stricken then and clambered down as fast as I could, literally putting my foot in something as I did so: 'How long?' I stammered. 'How long was I up there?' I burst into tears in my father's lap.

And at that very moment I heard a strange tapping – tut-tut tut-tut tut-tut. It struck me with a force like thunder, shattering the deceptive calm of this once-pleasant evening. My father's silence plunged me into a sort of madness. But in the midst of my fear – and my guilt and shame at this crime whose effects would soon be public knowledge – I found the strength to go to my mother.

'Will I be little my whole life? Really?'

Mother put the remote control down for a moment and looked at my father. Then she fixed her eyes on me and informed me that, yes, there was indeed a good chance that I would never get any bigger.

'Why? Why? Why?'

'Well! That's the way it is and that's that!'

And to finish, she made me promise not to climb on the table ever again.

What value or use could this oath have now? The verdict had already been given. My actions had provoked direct and immediate consequences. Despondency, humiliation, resignation and anger furrowed my guilty brow. I put myself to bed straight away, without brushing my teeth, without even wiping away the tears that ran down my plump cheeks. I spent thousands of hours – an eternal number of days – in a silent panic, waiting for the inescapable contraction of my bones, the formation of putrid protuberances, the appearance of the first bump. I'd be like a Malagasy zebu, I'd have the cumbersome humps of a Tunisian camel. The princess of

Saint-Benoît, with her pigtails and pale pink hair clips, was about to be turned into a tropical pygmy with a sequined headband.

I never climbed on a table again. In the presence of dwarves – monstrous little beings trapped somewhere between an adult and child – I was filled at once with pity and horror, and often stopped myself from saying, with terrible empathy and dramatic resignation, 'My friend, I will soon be one of you!'

Years later, I still prided myself on having escaped the curse. And I became pitiless with those who had almost been my comrades in misfortune. I was like a climber who had narrowly dodged an accident that had been fatal for the rest of his group: I forgot that it was mere chance, a simple arbitrary stroke of fate. I shouted at all the dwarves I came across with practised indignation, 'You've only got yourself to blame. Why the devil didn't you buy a stopwatch? Get hold of a clock? An egg-timer even?'

Happily, everything becomes a distant memory over time and no dwarf has ever beaten me up. Perhaps indulgence, for lack of forgiveness, settles like a shroud over even the sharpest desires for vengeance and the liveliest frustrations. Maybe children forget the omissions of their parents. Of course some tenacious memories linger on, occasionally taking hold, swelling and whispering unspeakable ideas of rebellion to the heart. But we have an essential instinct for amnesty – the urge to forgive our parents. It's the only way that traumatized five-year-olds can get past three score years and ten without catatonic depression or expensive psychoanalysis.

However, on rue Descartes, parents torment their children twice as much as anywhere else. They know full well that, as they themselves once did, their children will sulk and start to hate them

… before forgetting their rancour and eventually repeating the same absurdities. An eternal cycle of horror.

And even if one or two children never forgive their parents, by the age that major slanging matches start, their parents will already be dead. There is no danger of any recompense. The begetters of bitterness continue to say whatever they want, whenever they want.

As they did that July. We were picking our first oranges in the vast garden surrounding the house, as we did every year. The abundant crop put me in excellent spirits. My father, as always, warned me not to eat the pips. But while all parents of sound mind might justify this ban by referencing the risks of choking, the Dessaintes, once again, employed their usual technique, this time with a serious additional revelation.

'Anyone who swallows orange pips will feel them start to grow inside their body, and they'll end up becoming orange trees themselves. That's the way it is and that's that!'

It goes without saying that I was generally extra careful, even when devouring the smallest segment. But that day, no doubt distracted by the explosion of heat and light that flooded the fruit garden, I accidentally swallowed several pips. I can still remember it as if it was yesterday. I immediately realized what I had done but said absolutely nothing to my family. In my infantile head, where every parental maxim was planted as gospel truth, I could already feel this new metamorphosis taking root.

It would start with a vague prickling sensation, a barely perceptible tickle. The tantalizing feeling of nature working its wonders within me; it would make me smile to myself all day long. But it quickly would become a splinter, disturbing my sleep and piercing through my fingertips, my earlobes and the thin skin of my bare feet. I would suffer in silence. Somehow or other, I would manage to conceal the fact that my belly was being torn apart by wooden shards and young buds ripening. But there would come a day when neither my hair nor my little spring dresses could cover up the branches laden with flowers, the juicy oranges and, eventually, the nests of insatiable weaverbirds and the stench of rotten fruit. I feared for my eyes, expecting at any moment a branch that would puncture them as if they were silk. One morning, when the metamorphosis was almost complete, I would not hesitate to throw myself at my father's feet: 'Forgive me, Father! Forgive me for not heeding your advice, for being a bad seed!' And as my face was covered in leaves and my tongue became as hard as the bark from the *bois benzoin*,[4] I would extend my arm – my entire trunk – one last time in an attempt to seek my parents' pity. 'Farewell, Papa, farewell!' My mouth would disappear under a branch before I could even ask him to pray for me. While some become oaks and others silver lindens, I was to be punished by the gods and transformed into a common orange tree.

Since this episode, I have cultivated a hatred for orange trees, citrus-flavour drinks and all those damn stone fruits. Nothing scares me more than a seed. I believe that all the children from rue Descartes are like me, petrified at the thought of coming across one of those sneaky little pips concealed in a juicy orange segment and ready to eviscerate you with its shoots. Once, some years later, I shouted at my dad and accused him of being a terrorist. He replied that no one had forced me to believe him back then and, completely absorbed by his umpteenth toothpick, ended the conversation with his usual 'That's the way it is and that's that!'

---

4    Tree whose bark can be used as incense or a remedy against skin conditions.

In other words, at the age of five-and-a-half, fully absorbed by sucking my thumb and with a teddy tucked under my arm, I should have sniffed out the mockery like a well-trained police dog! I should have identified the deception and doubted the only adults I knew! Better still I should have detected some sort of contradiction to their sermon! But the pertinent fact was lacking: children are unaware of such things as deceit or suspicion, they don't even know that tales exist. A prince is a prince. A dragon deserves to die. Every myth is a fact; all legends are ancient truths. Children's faith and love are boundless and lead to their downfall. They have only one altar – the truth – and two gods – their parents – upon whose omniscience and wisdom they rely. Yet the only thing your parents see you as is a little, credulous lump of flesh and the chance to exercise their own immense powers! But good luck trying to explain this child-psychiatrist mumbo jumbo to the Dessaintes!

I never had the audacity to hate my father, or anyone else for that matter. The very thought that, somewhere in the world, a human being might loath their parents filled me with both shame and resentment. The rage that was building up inside me was inflicted on oranges and other citrus fruits. I hate them – with their vicious seeds and blinding zest – so much that I have stabbed hundreds of them until their orangey sap gushes out. Or I sink my nails into them and skin them alive. The luckiest ones end up slowly macerated to death in a flask of homemade rum; the rest are mixed with horse manure and used as compost on our neighbour's vegetable patch. But eat them? Never again!

I wouldn't hesitate to describe this period as a happy one though: children are satisfied with very little. And on rue Descartes, a little goes a long way. A tyre, two sticks, a few tales about haunted houses, a jug of water, and children feel like they have the world at their feet. If, on top of that, your mother doesn't make you wash behind your ears every week, you're as happy as Larry and he's as happy as you.

I suppose that when it comes down to it, these two bogus adults I was forced to call my 'parents' had nothing to offer me but their own terror.

On rue René-Descartes, the world left children with little choice. Dare to whistle at night-time? A monster would come and carry us straight off to a damp, dark lair where it would tear off our fingernails one by one, sprinkle a handful of salt over our fingers and then run water over them. Dare to snivel? Sitarane, an insatiable blood-guzzler, would be doing his rounds, and his particular favourites were little whiners with hair clips. Play out on the landing at dusk? Grand-mère Kal[5] was certain to be hunting then. In their capacity as wise and experienced adults, time and again, the Dessaintes would sit me on their lap and patiently recount the misadventures of our family and its numerous dead infants. The babies that should have grown up to be my aunts and uncles, if it hadn't been for a little stroll they took after six o'clock, an unfortunate noise they made, a few tears they shed – some small transgression that had prompted the devil himself to wring their necks. I was convinced by the descriptions of the dry snap of bones breaking, the image of a face turning blue and the eyes bulging in the head. A visit to the cemetery the following morning to see the seventeen small graves dispelled any doubts I

---

5    Monstrous creature that no Reunionese has ever seen, but that everyone can more or less describe. Definitely a toothless old witch with immeasurably long, very sharp nails that are ideal for slicing up little girls.

might have held; I vowed to be a model child for the next twenty-five years. To ensure that my submission would last forever and that their crazy stories remained secret, my parents swore that the long horns of a sacrificial goat[6] would sprout from my forehead if I dared repeat anything I was told to anyone. This same oath was imposed on all the children in all the districts in the entire island.

So the whole of La Réunion knew, but no one spoke about it publicly. And despite this silence nobody thought about anything else from morning till night; taboos unfailingly create obsessions.

Apart from in the seaside resort of Saint-Gilles, where the Europeans had succeeded in creating a pocket of atheism, a supernatural atmosphere where Grand Diab and Bébête Toute roamed freely had full reign. The sight of many Tamil temples and scarlet ribbons, of bags left at crossroads and of other occult practices – all underscored by the blood-curdling stories we were told – provided irrefutable evidence.

Perfect parents only exist in movies, but my silences, my nightmares and my fearful tears perhaps persuaded mine that they were, at least, excellent storytellers. So they hadn't failed at everything in life.

My sources are uncertain, but I have heard that there was a time when the Dessaintes were happy and good. When they dreamed of lullabies and well-behaved children, of embroidered baby clothes – of a second child with chubby cheeks to stroke. But nobody ever witnessed those days of tenderness and walks in the park, of a smiling child and of eternal 'becauses'. At first my parents never

---

6   Animal used in sacrificial Hindu ceremonies. To the great despair of animal protection organizations, the goat's head is cut off in a single motion from top to bottom using a well-sharpened sabre.

had time for that. Later, tomorrow, the day after tomorrow. Then it was too late. They had neither the will nor the way. What good would it serve? Wasn't it enough to have a full stomach? Finally, like all those in rue Descartes, they ended up appeasing their conscience by convincing themselves that they were good parents because their kid had a meal on the table every evening.

My uncertain sources even claim that the Dessaintes laughed once, on one occasion. Or smiled at least. One of those smiles that comes from a tender nowhere, somewhere human, possibly nervous. Though nothing is certain, to be honest.

What we do know is that destiny turned against them. In retaliation they tattooed a permanent sulk on their lying faces and spouted horrific stories and vicious barbs from their mouths when I dared to approach them.

―――――――

It all began one evening in 1981 in the town of Sainte-Marie in the north of the island, when two young people had the misfortune to meet.

At the back of a restaurant a cook removed his jacket and the white chef's hat that he had been wearing since morning. The fourteenth of July celebrations were in full swing outside. With his shift finished, the cook said goodbye to the head waiter. He crossed the dining room where several guests were finishing their dinner, putting his hand in his pocket and running his finger along the solitary banknote that his boss had been willing to advance him. He thought that perhaps it was high time he changed his life – or perhaps it was time to go home and sleep.

He left the restaurant, walking slowly along the sooty streets under an empty sky. As was the case every Sunday, he found himself very much alone in an immense urban universe. But as he came down towards the old town, he heard something unusual. It might have been described as the rumble of feverish voices. Another of those revolting choirs of drunks, he thought. But as usual, he was wrong.

At the crossroads, which had been deserted when he was there several hours earlier, he encountered a bustling crowd of young people. They were coming from all directions, dressed up and heading towards the loud music of the big dance. Then he remembered. It was the fourteenth of July!

The coastal districts were engulfed by a gigantic human tidal wave, merry, laughing and buzzing with life. Sometimes in small groups, sometimes as a huge swell, it swept towards the town hall, where the party was being held. This was not one of those little parties arranged by rural schools – this was the big beanfeast! The one time a year you defied your family's rules, the time you'd run the risk of paternal rejection and face down the fear of being disinherited – this was the time you might meet someone new.

Buoyed by the unexpected delight of the giddy crowd, the young cook removed his bitter mask and took sudden pleasure in strolling through the unusually bright and lively streets.

Caught up in the whirl of people, he even lost his head a little. Like those cowboys in films who lose patience as they wait their turn in saloons, he slowly hitched up his trousers, spat out a few insults – which were returned a hundredfold – and eventually succeeded in elbowing his way onto a calmer road, where some children, hidden behind a sheet of corrugated iron, were amusing themselves by launching bush passionfruit and velvet beans at the horde of passers-by. Taken by surprise and with his ears ringing, he took off once again and, without really knowing where his little legs were taking him, turned to the right into avenue des Amoureux. In a line of parked cars with their doors or windows wide open, he saw the quick movement of a gossamer skirt here, made out a blouse there – a bosom heaving beneath it. He heard stifled laughs, voices rising distinct from a sea of groans, and farther away, music from a car radio. Hot under the collar, he hugged the walls, caught between the cut stone and the overexcited young girls. It all made him keenly regret having only an old Gospel and an alley cat for company. The cat's scrupulous silence left him melancholic on southern winter evenings.

As he glanced about him – lipsticked lips, naked shoulders, and a troupe of lucky young men kissing them licentiously – a thought struck him. What if, like the hundreds here, he went to the dance that evening? Who knows, perhaps he'd find a sweetheart?

Up to then, Fate had been unkind. It was already an era of difficult girls and systematic rejections, and the tenacious odour of fried food and the smudges of grease that usually adorned his clothes didn't help. Fortunately, the day before, he had invested the last of his savings in two frivolities: a small bottle of *eau de cologne* and some brand-new trousers. He was wearing both that Sunday. Whistling a slightly saucy tune, he discreetly sniffed his armpits and headed for the town hall. Several minutes later, he found himself passing through the arbour of bougainvillea and frangipani flowers that formed the entrance to the dance.

What he saw there was merely a variant of the bawdy get-togethers organized on Sunday afternoons at the fire station. Years later, his solitary old age would make him mawkish and sentimental: he would remember it as a pure garden of roses, dahlias and ferns, where couples fooled around as their shadows waltzed across the walls.

People embraced each other in the large green space, or whirled around to the sound of the accordion. Elsewhere, the first disputes – caused by amorous rivalry – split the air. The firefighters, resplendent in their uniforms and complete with epaulettes and stripes, made the appropriate reproachful noises, but a minute later they had forgotten the ferocious bloodbath going on at the foot of the table. They pointed at the most tantalizing women, smoked cigarettes and roared with laughter in between the death threats. *Nunc est bibendum.* Cheers!

The party was going well.

Analysing a turn of phrase or assessing the elegance of a pair of large hoop earrings made of white gold, the girls tried to guess what town another was from, what match a second might aspire to, and which rich landowner from inland a third might be related to. The war was at its height, and they gathered in small groups on the wooden benches, believing that this was the best place to attract attention.

Next to them, fathers in tail-coats kept an eye on the procession of nymphets. Carried away by nostalgia for their own years of dancing, they sighed repeatedly and cheerfully, wondering whether they could still seduce one of these *Cafrines*[7] sipping on strawberry syrup and lemonade.

---

7   Reunionese woman of African origin. Subjectively considered the most beautiful and intelligent women on the island.

They were all keenly aware that the fourteenth of July marked the end of their paternal omnipotence. In a few hours, their much-loved daughter would tell them that she wanted to get married and, before they even had a chance to take out their whip, would laugh in their face and take off to live with a *Cafre la soie*[8] in a badly starched shirt.

After an entire lifetime of abstinence, our cook was now faced with a wide display of soft, perfumed flesh. He floundered, flinging himself headfirst at a small blonde in an azure dress with frizzy hair above her shoulders.

It was for this that he received his first slap at the age of twenty-one. It was as abrupt as the ending of his passion, but left the imprint of a strong, slender hand on his right cheek. In one blow, everything was extinguished: his hope, the volcano's fire, the lighthouse of Sainte-Suzanne, the blue moon and its blaze of stars, the happy voices of the celebrating town. Absolutely everything. The young man found himself rejected; alone once again on the fringes of an opaque and complicated world. His tail between his legs, he made a sorrowful resolution – he would quit the cruel world once and for all.

It was at that very moment that he noticed another young woman. She was sitting alone at the entrance to the ballroom, and though she seemed as ugly as all the rest of them there was something kind about her. Her backcombed bun, her fingers clutching a lace handkerchief embroidered with rosebuds, her dress (which smelled wonderfully of *Soir de Paris*), her lowered eyes: they all added up to something chaste and childlike, something

---

8    Reunionese man of African origin who is very (too) particular about his appearance.

inspiring sincere affection. Despair often leads to folly: he made his way towards her. As a man of experience, he faced the inevitable rebuff with dignity, but instead he was greeted with a smile and an invitation. The gods were certainly very mischievous that evening! A few minutes later, they allowed him to take the trembling hand of his partner and together, enveloped in the cool breeze from the sea, they danced for ceaseless hours.

This was how their story began. A slightly tremulous invitation that was transformed into an evening romance by the mild winter, mutual affability and a singular stroke of luck.

Incidentally, despite the reticence shown by the fairer sex where he was concerned, the cook was not completely ugly. Let's just say that his face was like his country: rounded, covered in bumps, chapped, and planted with a tuft of dark hair. What else could you expect, in this savage and tormented land of exile, scorched by the Tropic of Capricorn sun? Now that he was dancing, he sneered at those girls with their vicious tongues who mocked his rugged looks. Now that he was dancing, he launched a stinging attack on those perfect aesthetic examples – white, blond, handsome – who filled advertising posters throughout the island. Handsome or not, this evening he was dancing. And how he was dancing! And that was that.

The accordion continued to play waltzes and mazurkas, and the hum of the crowd seemed to have fallen silent. Dazed by the swishing dizzying whirl of the dresses, he silently praised his good fortune. What are twenty-one years of impatience, of heartfelt agitation, of irrational worry, he thought, if they end up resulting in romance? Softly closing their eyes, he and his partner danced with such lightness and vigour that they hardly seemed part of this world.

At around half past eleven, to a cacophony of applause, bench scraping, peals of laughter and sorry 'ohs' and 'ahs', the brass band – efficiently led by the accordionist Maxime Lacaille – announced the final polka and the firework display.

Having had enough of the crowd, the two dancers left the floor side by side and strolled along the line of latanier palms. Several metres from the police station, where the river flows into the sea, they sat down on the freshly cut lawn. Suffocated by propriety, they wondered a little stupidly which of them would speak first. This went on for an eternity. Afraid of their own voices, they both simply looked at the full moon. It was pierced with coloured sparks.

The firework display had begun.

Emboldened by the explosion of colour that lit up the sky, and its eternal rival the ocean, they finally exchanged a few words – a name, an address. They were interrupted by a photographer covering the event who aimed his camera and, in a slightly mocking tone, promised that they would get prime position in tomorrow's paper with smiles such as those.

In the corny photograph taken that evening is a girl – who would soon become my mother – in a grey dress, wearing a hat decorated with goose feathers and a short veil that partially conceals her face. On her trembling shoulders is my father's velvet jacket. He is standing next to her, in a collarless shirt and nylon trousers.

It's strange.

They seemed happy.

Two weeks after the dance, a dark man with a pleasant but worried expression made his way round the block four times. He was almost bitten by a stray dog and forced to swear on three occasions that he was neither a bailiff nor a tax collector, but finally – based on directions from a neighbour whom all the residents quite justifiably referred to as 'Snitchy' – pushed open my grandparents' wooden gate. He had come to get his jacket; he was offered a chair and Mum's hand. He accepted both with a smile on his face – which in him expressed surprise and satisfaction in equal measure – as soon as the offers were made. It was the 1980s after all. The decade of quick marriages, bitter marriages, arranged marriages – but marriages all the same. Given that the year hadn't yielded any particular pitfalls or any gifts, Father thought that a wedding, which was neither one nor the other, would add a little spice to life – or at least give him some company in his chronic solitude.

Nobody told him, at this stage, that he would soon be the parent to a snivelling little girl. One who would hasten to disclose in detail the – incidentally very unremarkable – ups and downs of his life as a father in books and newspapers as soon as she came of age. He was a very poor mathematician and an even worse visionary. Based on a quick piece of mental arithmetic, he concluded that a dowry would take care of his meagre expenses. His flat, upturned nose was already enjoying the scent of clean linen, hot meals and freshly cut bouquets of flowers. A subtle bulge poking up under his waistband suggested that he'd thought a little about other things too. Despite the apprehension of his solitary heart and the failed marriages that he had seen so often, he pictured himself ordering a frock coat, trimming his beard and buying two little rings and bedroom furniture on credit.

Who was this man? Where were his parents? Nobody knew and nobody cared whether he preferred rice or macaroni, corn on the cob grilled or boiled. Checking up on someone's background, criminal record and financial affairs was thought to be the concern of the rich. So Father remained a friendly stranger, with no friends, no name and no clear identity. To simplify things, he was given the name of his in-laws and became a Dessaintes. He had a job, a gold tooth and an Afro. All the signs of a man of his time, and this was enough to make him a good catch. What is a good catch, after all? A man with no story. All the better! Nothing to say and nothing left unsaid. Their relationship was born out of silence – a non-story from which they thought they could spin an entire narrative.

Sitting opposite him, Mother was a bronze statue: a combination of shyness, anxiety and silent reptilian prudence. Father remembered only that, when he consented to the sacrament of matrimony, she had bitten her lower lip so hard that a trickle of blood appeared. As he would say, she was one of a kind: two apricots for breasts, veins that protruded as if she was being strangled with a shoelace, the chestnut complexion of an Arab thoroughbred, the gaze of a snowman, and braces that she would keep until the age of twenty-three. No one ever knew what was going on in her head, this they had in common. He did not find her repulsive – from behind he even fancied her.

Second last in a family of twelve offspring, four of whom had died before they were weaned, Mother had the uncomfortable fate shared by later children – she was considered a burden. Had she been the eldest or youngest, she would have been mollycoddled, spoiled outrageously and fed with cherry guava jelly while the rest of the brood were offered only bread and dripping. But she was the eleventh in a family of twelve – in other words, nothing at all!

Back in those days, only the children at either end of the brood would shelter the family from ills. The eldest was the reliable team leader and the youngest the ultimate wonder of this vile world. Each received the adoration of their parents and the forced respect of their siblings. They grew up sheltered from both the cane and the chores that Grandfather imposed on the other children (each morning, from 5:10 sharp). But above all, whether you came out first or last, you were assured a glitzy and memorable marriage! For the firstborn, a magnificent wedding was both tradition and duty. The honour of the family depended on it. They would get into debt for two or three years, mortgage the house, the ox-cart and even one of the other kids (provided the banker looked the other way), as long as it guaranteed a spectacular wedding. As for the youngest, their nuptials were to prove the neighbours wrong who'd been saying you were bled dry and debt-ridden after all the marriages you'd had to pay for.

But being second-last only afforded you a tiny share of your parents' love. The endless births that preceded you, and the emotional slump each invariably brought, were to blame.

Mother therefore received only dull attempts at affection, scraped together from the leftovers usually apportioned to a favourite beast of burden. During the first eleven years of her existence, her parents politely ignored her, preoccupied as they were by their other children. She went to school more out of constraint than conviction, didn't understand a thing and spent all her breaks running after her wide-brimmed vacoa hat.[9] The boys amused themselves by using it for a

---

9    The vacoa is a tree that grows near the sea and whose leaves are used to make hats and baskets.

ball, worrying it around the yard while honking like geese. Late in the afternoon, all alone, she would walk the five kilometres from her school desk to the beatings her father handed out. And on the poorly surfaced road, her stomach clenched with fear, she would pray that no blood-red car (the colour preferred by child abductors) would take her away from the quiet life she was intent on leading, no matter what.

She would arrive home, receive a slap as a welcome, plus two baby bananas or a piece of sugarcane, and get straight to work. But not homework! Nobody cared about that. 'Napoleon won't be the one milking the cows,' Grandfather shouted. Real work! Like feeding the poultry, cleaning the barn, spreading manure on the fruit garden. Then, and only then, could she rest. Sitting on the protruding roots of a mango tree, she would sort rice and peel sweet potatoes. She would use the peelings as characters for her own little stories about passionate love and princely weddings. At first, she promised herself that she would only marry a minor royal from a good family – a rich, robust, romantic, reassuring, risk-taking, refined redhead. Someone who was a bit of a dreamer, a bit arrogant, a bit rough, a bit of a bragger. In the breeze that caressed her nostrils she detected the waft of faraway places, and she heard a melancholic hum from the wind in the lemongrass. 'It's a sign,' she thought. 'He will come from far away and play the harmonica for me at sunset.'

A few Valentine's Days passed, but the regal musician was still nowhere to be seen and the mango tree would now only produce stunted, stringy, tasteless fruit. She didn't want to share the same fate as the mango tree, so she lowered her expectations – choosing a young flamboyant[10] instead. She was done with her

---

10  Tropical tree easily recognizable by its bunches of red flowers.

unrealistic juvenile fantasies! In light of the very limited choice in the neighbourhood, ruling out the lame, the rowdy, the barflies and the flatulists – in other words eighty percent of the eligible bachelors – she would make do with a pestle maker or a roofer. Her motto became: 'Anything but solitude. Anything but staying here.' So, in a last-ditch attempt, every morning from then on she would draw a line of kohl on her eyebrows and split her curly hair into two big flat plaits that she tied with a rubber band, wondering whether there was any life, any spark, *something* before death. Like those cigarettes hanging from the fingers of old people who watch others come and go by the roadside, she wore herself out waiting. She dreaded being defeated, being crushed by solitude. But deep down she obstinately imagined that somewhere out there she was loved, awaited and worshipped.

As soon as she was awake, her parents would shout orders: 'Lift this!', 'Polish that!', 'Move this!' They would treat the children like little servants to be rewarded with a bit of curdled milk on Sunday afternoons. Starved and voracious, each would lick their bowl meticulously and, with a degree of hatred in their eyes, stare at the drops of milk the youngest was sucking from its fingers. And then, on weekdays, each child would return to their hedge school,[11] their fishing net, their tinware, their sewing, whatever, wherever, as long as their parents saw that they were busy.

All week long, a machete in his hand, their father toiled on a plantation that had been forcibly reclaimed from the forest. There, he was growing vegetables for a fat white man called Verrières: two

---

11   From the French 'école marron'. School where the teacher would work for their own benefit, illegally, and often during the school holidays.

rows of onions, a patch of thyme, carrots, pumpkins, calabashes, tomatoes, cucumbers, hyacinth beans and big watermelons whose shape made you think of small dead planets. He threaded his way between the rows of lettuces as you would walk between tombs: hurriedly and somewhat ill at ease. In the evening he'd come home with two big aubergines, a few sponge gourds or a papaya, carrying them in as if they were trophies. One of the children would be waiting for him to appear at the bend in the road and would run to inform their mother, who'd quickly place a dish full of beans, two pieces of meat and a chunk of bread on the floor in front of a small wooden bench. There was hardly a word uttered, never a smile exchanged, but every once in a while my grandfather put his food aside to give one of his brats a good slap – their comings and goings alone were enough to anger him. It seemed he was born gnashing his teeth.

The children, accustomed to their father's wrath, would only complain softly; seeking out their mother, who'd be busy mending the old Bermuda shorts and dresses that were passed down from one year to the next. No gifts, no birthday parties and few cuddles. This wasn't the Verrières household, where the children, in addition to having pocket money and toys, would brag about getting everything they wanted from their parents. This was an abode of humble people. Simple, humble people who were still sleeping on straw beds surrounded by walls covered with old newspapers.

All of this happened in Sainte-Marie, and then Bras-Panon, very near Millemogom (which is also called Paniandy sometimes). But it could have been happening anywhere – in the Hauts de Libéria or in Dioré, near Saint-Leu or even in Villèle. The place did not matter at all. Neither did the people. On this island, back then, the

Blacks, the poor Whites also known as 'Yabs', and the Malabars, whose ancestors had come from places like Calcutta, all suffered equally.

Only after dinner would their father loosen up. In a less severe voice, he would describe to the eight children sitting before him the monsters whose shadows he glimpsed when he went to the fields at four in the morning – hanged monsters with swollen tongues, giant highway-bandits, creatures who were half woman, half fish. This was the children's favourite time, these stories told by the light of a kerosene lamp, the huge centipedes chasing around the wooden benches. They didn't hate their life. Or rather, they had learnt to love it, just as one is surprised to realize that one has acquired an affection for the smell of fuel.

From Friday (payday) onwards, life would take a completely different turn. Grandfather would come home drunk, a jug in each hand, and shout himself hoarse insulting his wife, children and poultry – calling them calluses, snake-headed burdens. And every weekend, after a frenzy as crazy as an electric eel, he would pass out, a final complaint dying on his lips. The same complaint, every weekend, for sixty years: 'Life's a drag!'

Much to everyone's amazement, however, for two weeks each year he would only consume fruit and water. The fasting period had come. He was no longer the abominable meat-eater from the East, but a fat, tropical caterpillar whose head or tail could be seen – it was never clear which was which – in the trees whose fruit he ate. Otherwise, he would be seen smashing open a traveller's palm[12] or a coconut tree with giant machete blows. After he was finished with

---

12   Tropical plant that looks like a giant fan ending with banana tree branches.

it, the tree would drop dead. Since the family entertained vague religious beliefs, he would then go and confess as if going on a pilgrimage – sober, in his Sunday best, slightly nervous.

'What sins bring you here, my son?' the priest would ask, placing his chubby fingers on his pot belly.

And old Dessaintes would confess everything: the beheaded cat that had eaten from his dish, the gun drawn because of a badly cooked blood sausage, his Albertine who had lost two more teeth, and the beehives of Jismy-Big-Nose that had been set on fire!

'Are we to endure it all? What about an eye for an eye? An eye for an eye!' he would shout loudly enough to make even the confessional grille shudder. The priest would forgive him no matter what and would urge him to read the Apostles, mumbling some prayer and reciting the rosary without realizing that my grandfather had left the church fifteen minutes before.

Once again, the blue and humid earth would absorb the fits of anger, blasphemies and expletives of this walking bundle of nerves for a whole year. Once again, he would eat only fruit for two weeks, more out of concern for his cirrhosis than out of Christian fervour.

One Ash Wednesday, however, his conscience kicked in as he reread the Book of Matthew. 'Divine love is just and was given to all Men. […] Without love, there is no paradise.' From then on, my grandfather got it into his head to love absolutely all his children, including his second-last, and he took her out of school. A true Christian education could only properly be found working in the stables and at the washtub. Eleven more years went by and all her siblings had had the chance to escape – that is, get married. At the age of twenty-two, once her domestic virtues had been deemed acceptable, it became high time to offer them to a new household where, in turn, she could preach order, submission and equity to a long line of children. They just had to find the ideal husband – or rather, a willing one. Once again, they turned to the wisdom of the old apostle, whose text was being carefully reread at the precise hour that Father came knocking at their door. And because the door is opened to he who knocks, with no knowing what he was doing my grandfather welcomed in a future that would make the New Testament look peaceful.

A week later, my parents were married.

———————

Judging by the multitude of photographs exhibited in their sitting room over the following months, they considered the wedding a success. The same woman appeared again and again in the oblong frames: small, dark-haired, expressionless, rigged out in a stiff wedding dress, a cheap headband clasped around her head. My father, who at barely twenty-one was already holding his belly in, had managed to squeeze in between her left arm and the edge of the frame. As was the case with the four other weddings celebrated that day, after a brief walk down the aisle, they had blindly complied with the most worn-out social conventions at the church altar. There had been a scramble for portraits at sunset with the calm, blue ocean as a backdrop, then in front of every waterfall that appeared along the path of the wedding procession, and later in the fiery golden savannah, surrounded by a flock of kids who had come from God knows where, and last but not least, in front of the wedding cake sipping from each other's champagne flutes, their arms entangled like small, clumsy snakes.

Curled up on the sofa that had a view of the town, each morning before going to school I would look at the wall and this totally kitsch mise-en-scène, with its artificial flowers, paste jewellery, fake diamond necklaces and oversize limo (which had cost an arm and a leg – there was a rumour that, because of it, they had to serve rough plonk from Cilaos instead of Champagne and everyone had ended up with heartburn).

The icing on the cake was one last photograph where the young bride bent backwards from the waist simulating a plunge into rapture – her eyelids half closed, her hair ruffled like the crest of the red-whiskered bulbul. It was supposed to be like the cover of *Mariage & Délice* magazine, but what might have been graceful on glossy paper came across like an old flour sack in a cheap frame. She looked like the Tower of Pisa about to collapse onto the groom's over-polished shoes! But what did it matter? The guests were all happy and Grandfather even shed a tear on their wedding day. Love conquers all. *Amor omnia vincit!*

The banquet, as Reunionese tradition dictated, was held in the restaurant where Father still worked. On the previous day, long wooden tables flanked by hastily constructed benches had been set out on the terrace for the party area. At the start of the evening, a hundred cars poured through the heavy gates. Every parking space, every bed of herbs and every daisy bed sustained an onslaught of worn tyres; ruthless high heels advanced, stacks of fluorescent gifts piled up – a tower of ungainly packages, with pan handles or the ears of a Chinese pressure cooker sticking out of them. Twelve months of gardening wrecked by one wedding and two attempts at parallel parking! At the sight of the chaos, the attendant let out a cry like a sick beast. If it hadn't been for the arthritic torment that paralysed two fingers on his right hand, he would have stuck them into the eye-sockets of one of those showy guests – he knew they were slightly worse for wear and didn't even have driver's licences, let alone insurance.

'I hope this isn't a problem? All the spaces are taken and we're late.' He nodded or perhaps shook his head, but it no longer mattered. People were already parking their cars at an angle on his orchids and crushing his cacti the way you might stub out a cigarette. A procession of loafers and high heels then tramped into the restaurant and covered the floor with soil and bits of dead plants.

The day of the big feast had arrived!

In the space of one night, the restaurant, usually so quiet, was turned into a veritable beehive – hundreds of couples with their children (and their naughty habits) were buzzing around. But at least they had left their dirty mongrels at home.

The guests, greater in number than anticipated, arrived joyful and pot-bellied. Many of them had skipped lunch and were now hungry for anything they could get. They stamped with irritation in front of the narrow entrance that led to the reception room where an amateur photographer was capturing their nervous, impatient faces. At this stage, everyone was still with their family – clean-shaven faces, impeccable hairdos, quiet children. Nothing in the rustling of the evening dresses, the constant whispers of the impatient couples or even in the heady scent of aftershave hinted that a category-five hurricane was on its way.

As soon as they entered, the guests ran to the newly-weds to offer awkward compliments and fervent best wishes. The most generous put a half-sealed envelope in the wedding basket. The others piled up gifts on a wobbly sideboard – household linen, porcelain dishes, a chopping board, a salad spinner, even a pillow. They then sat down at a table, waiting for what they hoped would be a copious dinner while assessing how long the couple – destined to either break up or stew in the acrid waters of frustration and resentment – would last. Their gossiping was fuelled by jealousy: only their own happiness could possibly be authorized – they scoffed at the luck of others. Everyone, in reality, is only liked in proportion to their misfortune. While speculating about the number of children the couple wanted, each guest was imagining the inevitable mishaps, the inescapable storms that would turn the newly-weds into modern-day Jobs. They saw the happy couple sitting on the ashes of their burnt lives, eaten away by pustules of disillusion, deprived of their friends, and embittered or divorced.

And these prophecies were eminently plausible: Grandfather, gnashing his false teeth, had already been forced to acknowledge six divorces among his kids; each guest's own experience of failure in this area confirmed their predictions. Their failures weren't for nothing – they could warn other people now, become advocates of celibacy, inveterate debauchery, or permanent bigamy. When this couple failed, just as they had done, it would seem like a consolation. More sailors for the ship of fools, all those who thought they'd got a mermaid but had ended up catching a cod. These guests, slightly high on *zamal*[13] and as drunk as could be, shared the same loud and muddled thought: marriage was the vilest scam of all! Were it possible to turn back time, even if they were promised ten million francs, they wouldn't bite! The honeymoon period lasted a few weeks, at best three months, but then the lack of privacy gave way to

---

13   The local cannabis.

disappointment, the first cracks appeared, and a dull routine began – over and over again for eternity. The gaping wound of happiness was slowly and surely covered by a cold scab of mutual hatred. And then, who knows? Strangulation? Gunshot? A pot of boiling oil? Even if these dramatic methods weren't used, the result would be the same. On the surface, a respectable couple of good standing with virtuous children, but in less than five years each would exasperate the other, sigh with disappointment as if they were on their deathbed, and start to keep an eye out for something else. The men are usually the first to leave: Monsieur goes out every weekend and, once or twice a year, grants himself some respite in a Thai or Malagasy brothel – all the time pretending to have a new-found interest in Romazava stew, the Tsingy stone forest or pineapple rice. At the end of the year, this disorganized amateur traveller returns to La Réunion, and subjects his bare feet to firewalking as a sporadically pious Hindu. Six months later, with money stolen from the youngest's savings, he does the same thing all over again.

Madame, on the other hand, swells with despair. She can constantly be found sitting in her kitchen, taking care of children now in their forties, and excusing their laziness, bad manners and antisocial behaviour by pretending they have undiagnosed autism. By now she is generally in a state of extreme jealousy and irritability: burying her own desires she sees every woman as a rival, especially her daughters-in-law. She calls them all silly girls and, desperately seeking a distraction now her children have officially left home, she falls head over heels for a little dog and names it something like Actarus, Youki, Titoune or Excalibur. Having found her final life partner, a suitor faithful to a fault and beyond reproach, she loves the dog madly – so much so that on her deathbed her only wish is that the dog be taken care of. 'No dog pound! That's out of the question!' she implores the priest (who is more preoccupied with finding a chair for the late arrivals there to witness her final departure). This was the best-case scenario for marriages celebrated on rue Descartes and involving members of the Dessaintes family. But, in any case, it reflected the gloomy and prosaic nature of the era where the weekly feasts at least allowed people to eat their fill.

The guests were nervously fiddling with the paper tablecloth on the long wooden table and, like ill-mannered children, were overturning their glasses on the woven table runner, speculating about whether the meal would be a buffet or à la carte.

They would have kept up with these idle conjectures if Father hadn't interrupted them with a speech. For most of them, it was the first time they'd heard his monotonous voice. Mic in hand, he launched into a long oration, but the happy crowds only listened to the last three seconds – the important bit: Thank you. God. Love. Enjoy your meal. Mother wanted to read a poem she had written for the occasion. It was about a wide-brimmed hat, a mango tree and a wedding that made up for everything else. No sooner had she started than she was greeted by a thunder of applause and approbation. That dealt with that. Father resumed the air of a meditating monk and, speaking only to his wife, waited impatiently for bedtime. The formalities were over and now everyone was free to do what they wanted.

*Dominus nobiscum!* May the Lord be with us!

Everywhere you looked there were small groups of women bitterly passing remarks on this one's leopardskin tights or that one's fuchsia miniskirt. Everywhere you looked there was a procession of heavy hips and haunches like joints of meat, adorned in flashy colours –

predominantly blood red or bright yellow. Everywhere you looked were low-cut bodices, swollen with breasts as round as melons, bare backs crossed with bra-straps, black lace dresses with the tag from the laundrette hanging from the hem. When the women bumped into each other, they asked the same questions: 'Where do you live now? How many children do you have?' They would then show each other their children – to hide the absence of everything else, to justify the twenty-three kilos they had gained that year and excuse all the missed communions, picnics and nights out.

The men, in short-sleeve shirts, were clustered in front of the alcohol table, indiscriminately helping themselves to more beer, glasses of whisky, cheap wine or rum, which they liked to add salt or lemon to. At times they discreetly left the room and went in small groups of three or four to pee against the wall and pass around a joint. They then returned to the buffet, louder, sprightlier and more talkative than before. Under the hum of the general noise, they proudly described the remarkable adventures of their exciting lives. They all thought they were sex on legs, and they were all extremely popular with women – especially *tantines la roue*[14] and the beauty salon dolls, all fascinated by their rugged beauty and their virile intelligence. Their ever-changing audience would laugh until they wept at the ribald gestures they used to illustrate their tales: their wedding night, their latest infidelity, a drinking bout, how they'd captured the tenrec in yesterday's hunt.

Never had they had so many anecdotes to tell! Never had a wall heard a woman scream so loudly on a honeymoon! No one could

---

14   Expression referring to a woman who is attracted to men with very large cars.

handle the mix of Dodo beer, homemade rum and cane liqueur as well as they could! Never had another man and his faithful mongrel endured such perilous full-moon hunting expeditions. Even if they had returned empty-handed – or at best with three tenrecs and a palm heart[15] – they had braved two-headed cats, six-metre-long boa constrictors, Lom-Kok[16] and will-o'-the-wisps who, with their hand on their liver, they swore they had seen up there, in the Plaine des Fougères – unless it was behind the arum lilies of Piton de l'Eau or near the old abandoned mill in the Makes forest? Those endless weddings, they were all different, yet all the same. They were all failures.

In the middle of the crowd were the children, their shirts crumpled, their foreheads sweaty, their bow ties buried deep in their pockets. They had been set loose and now scurried about like gangs of scorpions. They wobbled the tables with their dirty hands, burping as loudly as they could. They burst the balloons, knocked over their half-empty plastic cups onto the paper tablecloths, and ran over the flower beds to pluck the leaves from a bergamot tree. They held a contest to see who could spit the farthest. Bored at last of their stupid games, they came back to sit at the table and spent their time yelling, into the total indifference of the crowd, 'So-and-so farted! So-and-so farted!'

The elderly, sitting in a dark corner, waiting for dinner and death, spoke only of Father Pedro and Abbé Pierre. When they grew tired of those mournful conversations, their hands buried in their

---

15　Consumed cooked or in salad, this is a refined dish that is much prized in La Réunion.

16　A mysterious man with a cockerel head. He was rumoured to go chasing after children in the west of the island. [Translators' note.]

winter coats, they planned what they would get up to in heaven, or perhaps the next day, after the festivities.

Around nine o'clock, the guests were served handfuls of over-salted peanuts, green olives from Tunisia, biscuits whose crumbs stuck to your fingers, cold and mushy samosas that had been at their best in the afternoon, a few brown and shrivelled cocktail sausages, shredded cabbage, crusty chicken and white bread on cardboard plates. Then came fish curry, chicken masala, bean stew, jasmine rice served with a green pepper puree and a salad of lettuce sitting in a pool of white vinegar and sunflower oil.

Initially, the guests sought to reflect the good manners they had been taught at school; they took up their forks, aligned their knives and elegantly tucked in their napkins above their pussy bows or lace ties – God knows who they thought they were imitating. But the stainless-steel cutlery and refinement were very soon dispensed with. Inspired by the instincts of the person next to them, the guests began to openly use their hands instead – all the time demanding more and more sauce and extra pepper. Because after all, on these rocky shores lapped by the Indian Ocean, eating with your hands, feasting and dancing barefoot to the rhythm of a *roulèr* drum was far superior to wearing trousers with braces and dancing a dull tango in some dodgy open-air dance bar by the Marne River.

Surrounded by the usual din, improvised drinking contests began. Everyone called out to one another – 'Té, cousin!' – intimating a warm friendship. They were delighted to be there but their memory betrayed them; they couldn't even remember a nickname as ordinary as 'Dédé'!

Once they had feasted, tipsy and clutching their umpteenth liqueur, the majority waddled into the dining room, which had been transformed into a dance floor. A disc jockey (paid in cash upfront), operated the mixing desk and the light show while eyeing up a young Dessaintes girl of twenty who was twisting her hips and squealing like a dolphin on a downer under the rented disco ball. Further away, several women were swapping their high heels for flats or dancing barefoot, while the oldest of them, numb with cold and boredom, were installed on wooden chairs. They were keeping lookout for the arrival of the cake, coffee and cream puffs. The dancing went on for hours to the sound of *maloya*, Mauritian *séga*, *soukous* and *zouk*. Everyone swayed their hips: right to left, front to back, low to high. They hadn't moved like that since that christening last summer, but they couldn't hold still anymore. At the climax of this unbridled night, shouting 'yeah, yeah, yeah,' they spontaneously arranged themselves into a long single file, and wound their way through the kitchens, between tables and pushchairs – nearly knocking over the newly married couple and overturning half the benches and plates. The DJ, unsettled by this overexcited conga on one side and by the equally overheated young Dessaintes girl on the other, suddenly cut the music and the light show. He claimed he had an urgent need to use the bathroom. Fortunately, the overwrought crowd calmed down and went off to find a glass to drink from. It didn't matter which glass – they were all brothers at this hour – and it didn't matter what, as long as it wasn't water. Once the DJ returned, they embarked on a series of mawkish slow dances and *zouk*-loves. The men's shirts were open down to the navel and they held their wives tight. They had a vague memory of having loved these women – they were not that ugly, not that bad, not that fat after all.

This was the moment chosen for the highlight of the event: a thick shower of confetti that lifted every arm and face to the heavens.

They were all overcome by euphoria! Bathed in this paper snow, and the laughter it drew from even the most sombre of couples, they completely forgot all the church obscenities about the benefits of celibacy and the ideal of chastity. What a wedding!

Once again, the dancing starts. Once again, the disc jockey orders the children not to run under the tables. Once again, the guests request the songs *Cent pour cent* and *Le Minou à la voisine*. And Grandfather, his snub nose like that of a small rat, struts and scuttles through the delighted crowd with an air of 'I told you there was more to come'. People congratulate him as he passes and then go back to dancing or clinking glasses, while the bride and groom, seated in immense white rattan chairs, drink their umpteenth glass of demi sec sparkling wine.

Outside, the top lip of one female guest – first heir apparent to Miss Cherry Guava – has just been split. A brawl is breaking out. She's removing her heels, quickly fastening her hair into a bun and rushing to tear out Mireille's. Nobody knows how it all began. What's more, no one even knows who this Mireille is and where she comes from. The only thing that can be gleaned is that the former is said to have stolen the latter's husband, one Sunday in April when their children were hunting for Easter eggs together.

'*Ma arrache ton plime, espèce ti piment!*'[17]

Straight off the bat, the wannabe beauty queen attacks her rival with her stilettos. Cheered on by a crowd of honest women, she targets the weasely eyes of this headcase, almost regretting not having seduced her father and her two brothers as well. Mireille doesn't back off. She too removes her heels, jamming one in the

---

17   'I'm going to tear out your hair, you little pepper!'

young woman's teeth and using the other to hit her in the face, which is caked with cheap foundation. With a black eye like that, she can kiss goodbye to the Miss Strawberry competition next month. The eyelids of one are already puffed out, the other has a split lip, but the beating and shouting continues.

'Shark! Locust! Old nag!'

'*Espèce ti pitain!*'[18]

Nobody wants to separate them; it doesn't even cross their minds. Inside, the music is still going strong. A circle of dancers forms. The guests enter it one after the other and do a few dance steps, a boisterous *maloya* playing in the background: a couple of pirouettes or a glissade, finishing on their knees, their arms wide open. The wannabe beauty queen is now flat out on her back, being dragged along by her hair, winded and beat. Her favourite song, but she hardly hears it. She's struggling like a fat ladybird that can't flip itself back over. Mireille drags her several yards, repeating the same phrase:

'I told her I'd tear her hair out one day!'

Gone are the affectations and simpering airs from the start of the evening. At this late stage of the dispute, one has chipped nail varnish, while the other's skirt is torn to shreds. They each have only one shoe.

Wearily, several women finally separate them. A new set of *ségas* has begun and the gentlemen are looking for partners! Blouses are adjusted, red lippy reapplied, and the women return to the dance floor as quickly as they left it, remarking at how all this refreshens the appetite.

--------

18  'Dirty little whore!'

A few hours later comes the ordeal of the dessert: a wedding cake consisting of five tiers of choux puffs, decorated with arabesques, wafer flowers that have now wilted, and pink and blue ribbons. Just like the dole office, a long queue of half-asleep people forms, snakes its way towards the choux puffs and smacks two kisses on the cheeks of the bride and groom in exchange for a paper plate that contains a piece of the cake – a bizarre confection of liquorice syrup, soursop puree, preserved loquats, creamed red kuri squash, salted jackfruit and caramelized jujube. Nobody knows exactly what it is, only that it's bad. It is time to serve the coffee and lukewarm sparkling wine.

At around four in the morning, the drunken parents leave the dance floor and set off unhurriedly to look for their children. They bend down and extract one or two from the heap, looking them right in the face to make sure they are theirs. But they're in a total muddle. Once they've realized their mistake, they clumsily replace the children. Four are sleeping on a bench, three others in baskets strewn with soothers. Some have succumbed to sleep as if they were sitting in school, their heads lolling on the table next to empty bowls, gold streamers and a little net bag of sweets. One infant, half covered in a purple woollen blanket and woken by the noise, is watching with wide, fearful eyes as the drunken bodies roam around his pushchair. Some lean on it casually for support, while others lose their balance and shunt into it.

Once they have located their offspring, the parents toss them over a confetti-covered shoulder like a large sack and stagger towards the car, a three-quarters-empty bottle of whisky under their arm. Nobody goes with them. Nobody sees them leave. At that hour, the young bride and groom, a thin line of dribble slithering across their chins like a grass snake, are sound asleep in the white sheets of their hotel bed. Their party is a success. The die is cast.

———————

The next day, the two strangers handed in the key to their suite an hour late and set off for Saint-Benoît, a coastal town with no history. They settled there in a well-populated neighbourhood, on rue René-Descartes, at the mouth of the Marsouins River. From its hard, greyish stone, they built themselves a home that they intended to be solid, immovable and hardy enough to withstand the capricious weather. The house still exists.

Bordered by the road to the north and the riverbank to the south, the rectangular dwelling stands on an immense plot of semi-cultivated, semi-wild land that smells of frangipani and wet earth. April is still the best season to wander around there, when the sweltering heat gives way to the humid scent of bark impregnated with green moss. Time itself seems to slow, tangled up in a confusion of creepers and branches weighted with fruit – heavy-hanging fruit set down like an offering on the squelchy earth.

What happened there was just an incredibly ordinary story starring two ageing adolescents. Though they were unaware of it, the burst of energy as they came together created a mirage that tore them from their infinite solitude and languor for a whole three months. The world became a vast expanse of promises and optimism, where elation and love were one and the same – a mighty sphere with neither fissure nor seam.

These three months formed the bedrock of their memories.

Father worked every other day, and the money they received at their wedding allowed them to live like kings. They entered the modern world hand in hand: first car, first gas cooker, first advertisements, first loans. Shopping in a mini-market – a fan, a radio. To think that they had been sleeping on straw just ten years before!

'This supermarket trolley is so very fine,' they shouted as one. 'Let's take it home!'

Soon there were two abandoned trolleys in their backyard, one collapsed on its side and eroded by rust, the other missing its wheels. Each inherited the detritus of their happiness: two dozen empty beer bottles, bits of metal that might be sold for scrap, a coffee grinder, a few rags dried out by the sun, an old shoe.

---

Virtuous and intrepid, they rose at seven and larked around until ten, spinning a cocoon of bliss and good fortune around the house. Then they went to look for flowers, or seeds, or they just rolled about on the ground, marvelling at a dragonfly. Sometimes they longed to be butterflies and sometimes millionaires. 'How in love I am! I've loved you for three months already! Is there anything left to eat, my love? I'm going to work, but I'll come home soon so we can make love!' They wore lace. They ate strawberries, whipped cream, steamed dumplings, fruits in syrup, slightly crunchy honey and fried stuffed peppers in bed – a bed that creaked and creaked and creaked. Ten thirty. They held one another tightly. Eleven. They were invincible. Twelve already! They jump out of bed, they embrace, they laugh, they eat. Twelve thirty. No fatigue, no hunger, no need for a nap, no thirst. Nothing. Only vast ladlefuls of happiness. Only swigs of sweetness. A little more seventh heaven? Another helping of this ecstasy? What's it like to be loved this much? You tell me! No! You. Oh, no! You! I'll go wherever you go. You'll go wherever I go? We'll both go. You, us, us, you.

There was no end in sight!

In the afternoons, consulting a long list, they spent hours strolling around the nearest DIY store buying nails, wooden flooring and tiles. They returned home with a car filled with banal bric-a-brac and silly plants. An armchair, some artificial flowers, a small cat that moves its right arm, a collection of pin badges. At first, this was enough.

After a few weeks, finding the house too spartan, they placed cuddly toy animals in each room: in the corners of doorways, in the empty bookcase, on the sole bedside table, in the middle of the sofa – everywhere. Proud of their fun-fair fashion items, they smiled at their stuffed okapis, their baby tigers and rabbits, the same way you'd smile at a child.

But still there was something missing. So, beside the plastic anemones in their black plant-pots, they installed two small and sleepy tortoises, which vegetated on a bed of excrement, lettuce and solitude. They placed a television in the middle of the living room opposite the corner seat where they slept off their happiness. It was on in the background all day long – whenever they were there and even when they weren't – a stream of war reports, musical interludes, advertising jargon, cooking shows, a thousand ways to make your fortune, a hundred tips and tricks for becoming more beautiful; a report on deforestation, another on teak furniture, a final one on excess debt. Their happiness took the shape of a well-furnished little love-shack, with a small garden at the front and a large yard at the back – in return for three hundred and sixty in monthly payments. Every day they congratulated themselves on having made it.

In the restaurant kitchen where he very quickly returned to work, the good gentleman now whistled as he browned spices and drew small hearts in soy sauce on the rim of each plate. The good lady waited to fall pregnant, making cotton romper suits and little woollen bonnets, searching for the perfect first name.

In late afternoon, they dallied here and there – collecting overripe avocados, breadfruit, a guava with pink flesh. Weighed down by their harvest (from which slid the odd frightened caterpillar or slimy crumb of squelchy earth), they would then sit down on the bank. Feet interlaced, they recalled their brilliant wedding or watched the water in the river below flowing towards the ocean. Weaving a web of flattery about themselves, dazed with love and long embraces, they remained there, outside of time, until the sun, sated by the day, drowned itself in the sea. During the blue evenings of the southern winter, having drunk a little too much anisette, they exchanged sweet nothings 'For you, dear husband'; 'Dear wife, I will always adore you!' Each promised to have the first name of the other tattooed on their right shoulder as soon as they had more money.

A delicious shared life had begun. The weekdays passed in an amorous trance and the weekends were spent with the in-laws, at their houses or on a picnic. They felt like lords of all they surveyed as they arranged their china, got drunk and roared with laughter sheltered from the sun in large verandas, or under the palm trees by the Anse Waterfalls or the pepper plants at Bassin Bleu. Someone would seize a kayamb, another would sing, and the rest would dance themselves ragged to the joyful beat. Not that they were music connoisseurs, but the noise alone was enough to make them happy. The Shrew (yours truly) had not yet been born.

They slept, they dreamt, they woke and the dream continued. And this happiness, they thought, was just compensation for past hells: the dullness of childhood, incessant poverty, solitary adolescence – and their history, their traumatic history of chains and servitude that had held their pride captive for generations and turned them into violent beings. All that was behind them now.

Sons of Africa, sons of slaves; they had had enough of being sons! Nothing would ever weigh them down again. The present was full of wonder and was ruled by love.

———————

It is true that their ancestors were among those strong and wiry *Cafres* who were seen disembarking in Saint-Paul Bay one accursed day in the seventeenth century. To think they considered themselves lucky, after having overcome fits of insanity and anxiety, rape and torture, storms and scurvy! Terrorized and demoralized they may have been, yet they had no idea what was going to happen, not only to them but to their children over the course of two, four, even seven generations. Had they known, would they have immediately jumped into the raging sea? It was infested with sharks and filled with grief – and smashing the skulls of their blood brothers against the rocks nearby – but would they have plunged in nevertheless? Or – despite the weight of their iron chains – would they have run straight into one of those bayonets that was pointing out the path to civilization, piercing themselves through the heart? But they didn't know what awaited them. Nobody had ever returned to their native land to tell their story. Nobody had returned to say, 'Cut out your tongue with a razor. It's for the best! Impale your daughters on these burning-hot stakes. It's for the best! Cut off your penis and throw it to the dogs. It's for the best! And then kill yourselves. It's for the best!' They didn't know. There were rumours, but nothing certain. So they chose life. That is to say they chose subjection. That is to say torture, hell and then death. In any case, it all came back to exactly the same thing.

It was winter in the southern hemisphere on the day the slave ship spat out its cargo from the hold. Neither hot nor cold. Neither grey nor blue. A season that was half-alive, like them. Quickly gone, quickly forgotten. It was the first time most of them had seen the ocean. And now the coral earth, the small tortoises making their way to the sea, the western bay festooned with palm trees.

When they understood that something worse than the ship's hold could exist, they bade a discreet farewell to their wives and brothers, to the infants who'd had the audacity to survive without milk, without a mother, without anything. They were already regretting all the things that they hadn't said or done back home: love on the banks of the Couama; war against those cockroaches, the Yao; even those few notes that they had dreamed of composing on an old likembe.

Drenched with fatigue and sea water, wearing only loincloths around their waist, they had staggered onto the cold, black sand, hoping that this mountainous land would be, at the least, tolerable.

With pointed teeth and bound hands, they had respectfully bowed down before their new masters, only to be branded with hot irons. Forty piastres per Negro, a bit less for cripples. A discount if you take a job lot.

45

The initial silence was replaced by cries of panic. But after a few blows with a stick, servile resignation set in; they watched the stern of the ship moving behind the line of beefwood trees as it headed away for the cardamom plantations of India, for the porcelain markets of China.

If only they were all to remain together, as snug as the bodies in the graveyard ... But their saviour had decided otherwise: two Blacks from Congo, four from Mozambique and three from Tamatave. With enemies in the same hut, the risk of insurrection was low. There was no point in thinking of escape when a rival ethnic group would betray you. So they set about working, working and working some more. And they experienced their first cyclones; branches that hung down and swung like monkeys, that chattered as they twisted together. Then the humid heat, termites, malaria. One morning, they noticed that the youngest piccaninny was already twenty-two. A quarter of a bad century had passed.

Although some still dreamed of flat-bottomed boats slipping away at twilight towards their native land, most realized that they would be buried here, at best under a takamaka tree in between the foam and the mud. And so began the suicides, the psychotic disorders, the infanticides, the pennyroyal abortions.

The abyss calls forth the abyss.

For their masters, it was the time of clean slates. Everything was erased: the past, family, memory, god, music. And everything was reconstructed, starting with names. Gone were the unpronounceable anthropoid titles. In their place stood Nathaniel, Désiré, Françoise, Germain (known as Toto), Baptiste, Paula, Mario. It sounded better. And, in turn, these newly named people were forced to stutter the language of their saviours. They worked as servants, animal keepers, beasts of burden, village builders, wombs for pleasure. And Mulungu, the great deity who had been so recently venerated, took on the pale aspect of a thirty-something depressive with an old-fashioned tunic and greasy hair crowned with brambles. Their descendants would even go to pray to him from time to time at Notre-Dame-de-la-Salette or at the Virgin with the Parasol in Sainte-Rose. Chrissy, Christ, Christoff … they had difficulty remembering the first few times. Who cares anyway? It was a stupid name, whatever it was!

But once evening came they slipped their frizzy heads between the iron bars of the Negro cabin and looked up to the sky. They envied the large, free clouds and the multitude of stars, shooting off like fireflies towards the infinite horizon. Goddess, Mother Earth, save us!

Spurred on by liberty and a thirst for the unknown, some managed to run away. In the depths of the mild, blue nights, no one remembered the route they had taken. Nobody even remembered having left. All that mattered was running. Not looking back. They searched in vain for sorghum, passed by the stands of latanier palms, wandered for days between the whitish bark of the balata trees on one side and the thick forest on the other. But they found only the mountain, impassable ramparts, and the tenacity of the slave hunters – Dugain and Mussard, Bronchard and Caron. These nightmares were all they had to nourish them. So they returned home – or in other words to hell. One ear less, one fleur-de-lis more.

But a more fortunate few had reached the interior. Still terrified by the singular, awful certainty that hell was just behind them, the group plunged deeper into the bowels of the forest. Deep. Deeper and deeper still. From time to time they stopped and, chasing away the dancing clusters of tadpoles, bent their emaciated faces over a stagnant pool to drink the cool water. The world no longer held any value.

They were temporarily lost, but they were encouraged by the fact that there were no lions or black mambas. In a hidden valley, they took refuge. They built huts of latanier palms, surrounding them with hedges of song of India and oleander. For the first few weeks, they had hardly slept. Resigned to their inevitable defeat, they awaited the iron muzzle and the whip. The fangs of the dogs. A blade slicing through the back of the knee. Volleys from a pistol. They no longer even understood why they had fled, why they'd harboured that vague – that infernal – wish for liberty. They wished they were completely stupid or mad, or that they were brave enough to swallow the angel's trumpet and face a final emancipation – or to jump from one of those cliffs shot through with pointless waterfalls. They moved, looked down, moved again and were overcome by vertigo. They watched the days go by, one by one. Living was a lost cause; they would simply let the days go by.

It was in this state they discovered the ibis and the tough meat of the white-beaked coots; it was in this daze they grilled the flesh of the last fruit bats, which still glided through the vampire sky at nightfall. Despite themselves, they felt something. A barely perceptible scent, but it was there all the same. Pride. They were still fearful, still anxious, but above all they were proud. They had escaped.

And because love always survives, in the shells of the last giant tortoises they placed their first children – born in exile, born runaway slaves. Perhaps these babies understood straight away: they never arrived in the daytime but only in the dark depths of the night; they didn't cry when they were born. It was as if they sensed the shadows were their salvation and that making a noise was digging a grave.

On the breasts of these tiny, free people they placed a talisman made from those miniscule cowry shells that all at once recalled their country's currency, their forgotten river and their lost riches. This one would be called Anchaing, that one Aurère. He will be brave! He will avenge us all!

At the dawn of the nineteenth century, they dream of armed insurrections, collective emancipation, a Libertalia somewhere between Grand Bassin, the Rivière des Remparts and Roche-Plate. They give themselves names and etch them into their hearts like promises that are impossible to keep but can never be forgotten: Nyanga or Spartacus, Bréda and Ogé, Mambo (known as Fatiman). 1811: Élie revolts in Saint-Leu. 1817: Furcy claims his freedom. But, as always, history rampaged over them: they were still hunted down – tendons were severed, the cosh was brandished, the stake or the wheel awaited. Followed by more grind: coffee projects, acres of cane and finally freedom – that is to say further work, alienation and destitution. 1848: The abolition of slavery arrived too late. And the competition for work from indentured labourers[19] was bitter. After that, they were on the move from one plantation to another, they begot less athletic sons who caught the worst illnesses – dysentery, tuberculosis, cholera. 1869: These twenty-year-old boys looked like forty-year-old men. 1899: The first signs of collective amnesia. The names of those who were first to disembark are no

19  Indenture: colonial practice from the 19th and 20th centuries that consisted of sending labourers who were originally from Asia or even Africa to work in La Réunion.

longer remembered; no one even wonders about them anymore. 1914: War begins in Europe. Melancholy lingers in the tropics. Most succumb; they no longer wish to flee though they are free to go. This country has become their own; they have no other. Few will ever return home. It doesn't matter where you die; death is the same everywhere. 1941: Nothing. So what? 1947: Ditto. 1955: Their fifteen-year-old sons shout that they have had enough of being Black. At school, someone said that all Blacks are nothing, that they are worthless, that they do nothing. That even the harkis[20] are better. Apart from little Louis, whom everyone calls the white Negro and considers mad, nobody thinks it's worth playing with them. Being idiots like them. And so they only play with one another. 1968: A drop of pride remains in their blood – they create a collective to advocate for the recognition of the Black people of La Réunion. Jean Vaudeville receives them in the offices of the former India Company, which have become the administrative headquarters for the *département*. He is in a hurry. The major general organizes a large gathering within the hour. It's impossible to miss this official reception, full of the usual crowd of hangers-about. 'Yes! Yes! You too. You are the Republic!' 1969: A new prefect is appointed and the collective is banned. 'The Republic is not a hotel for flashy foreigners. Perhaps it is time for these egalitarian dark people to become civilized. What about assimilation? Have they considered that as an idea?'

Finally, the illustrious empire of bygone days, the gold of the Zambezi, and the huge acacias, only live on through a few rituals

---

20 Harkis: Algerian soldiers who fought with the French during the Algerian War of Independence. [Translators' note.]

and a little *maloya*. These final fragments of their defeated audacity are sung in secret once night has fallen, when the gentle breeze has cooled the dusty alleys, dried the sweat of the day and begun to turn the warm huts frigid.

By the time the 1970s rolled around the end was nigh. They had forgotten everything: their mother tongue, the words of the prayers they should address to their ancestors, their rites of passage. They confused the Limpopo and the Zambezi. Even the name of their native land. Everything had been lashed away, generation after generation, with violent blows of the whip.

All this notwithstanding, they had gone from huts to homes made from milled logs, and then to small wooden houses with corrugated iron roofs, where they lived on the dregs of people's pity, boiled rice and casava pancakes. They stored their food near their only source of light – a candle – above their charcoal stove. Madagascan and Malabar rituals lived on through them. Every day, the men were busy cutting cane, pollinating vanilla, scraping away at the earth on large inland estates or setting traps to capture Malagasy turtle doves. At around seven in the evening, each family carefully tidied away their sandals. They assembled around their father's workbench, drank from tin mugs and ate in silence. For fancy meals they ate tree tomato stew, chicken wings and white rice. 1980: The strapping athletes of yesteryear have become sluggish souls. They hardly ever make it past primary school. They sit at the back of the classroom, plagued by boredom. At first they tried their best to learn there and only yawn discreetly. Then they begin to lose heart: poor results pile up relentlessly, year on year. There's some refuge at the back of the class, where the summer air's less hot. But it's more difficult now to keep those yawns quiet; there's not enough space to stretch out the shoulder-blades. The schoolmistress screams at these 'complete cretins'; all these darkies half asleep, yawning and stretching their spines. Until the day comes when the engraving of a slave man-monkey on the cover of Colbert's Black Code is brandished in front of them and they're introduced to their proper place in the empire, and the drama of the servitude borne by their cousins and ancestors. Bunch of dummies, snorts the teacher, thank the government in Paris for being so charitable! After this class, their education is over. They will find some other way to get by on this rock that tastes of ashes and blood, where their fathers had never asked to be.

Any anticolonialist from another French territory would have been quick to evoke the learned inferiority complex, traumatic memories, perverse determinism, collective neurosis and vicious circles of violence – but here they only talked of a difficult end to the century, of a century on its last legs. And it was then, as the sun set on this shipwreck century, that my parents took it into their heads to be born, to grow up, to get married and to perpetuate their line.

––––––––––––

My own Dessaintes clan became too poor to remain honest, too proud to admit they were penniless. They were discreet people, even if they liked a gossip, and they loved watching TV for hours on end. They abided by the law when they had to, paid their taxes lest the bailiff should come knocking on their door. They complained a bit, as good French people do, but their knowledge of the world was delimited by their television screen. They possessed practical commonsense and some very basic reading and writing skills, which they sometimes put to the test while gazing into the daily newspaper at the headlines or the horse-racing reports, or at the crosswords section. As a result of all this, neither Monsieur nor Madame had an exceptional character, nor a mind creative enough to adapt itself to a happy and lasting life together. Five months and twenty days after their wedding, their pleasant life as a couple was covered with a thin layer of dust, and it began to show signs of decay.

On top of these fundamental personal failings, there came an economic downturn which, in all its cruelty, created a deluge of layoffs and debt throughout the country. All hope was lost, even for Saint-Benoît. If you were coming from the towns of the North and on the last descent of the road known around here as Bourbier-les-Hauts, you would catch a glimpse of the haphazard roofs of this large, lethargic hamlet. Your heart would be gripped by an icy chill at the sight of the office workers' ugly square houses, the abandoned petrol station, the church built by some lost Lazarists, a couple of banks with hardly any customers, a sickly mayor, and the shops that, one after another, had rattled down their iron shutters for good. And that was pretty much what the town amounted to. Everything seemed to be crushed by the same sense of inertia. Had it not been for the inhabitants' Creole accents, any visitor would have thought they were in Moselle, or Dunkirk, or not far from one of those mines in northern France where coal-dust had suffocated all the life in town.

Unemployment and extreme poverty. A few small elderly drunks here, some young loiterers there, women flanked by their broods of scrawny, yammering children elsewhere. The same words were on all their lips. They all feared and talked about the same things. And then the worst happened: Father lost his job as a cook. First, the restaurant started opening only for lunch, then only at the weekend. Then, two of the three cooks were laid off. Eventually, the owner decided to blame the lack of customers on Father – whom he considered a total loser with the ambition of a battered fish – and he shut his restaurant for good.

With his chef's hat now hanging on a rusty nail, Father carried his bitterness and wounded dignity from one job to the next, but he often came back empty-handed. Once – possessed by some reckless spontaneity – he had sworn, 'I will be a person of private means or nothing!' and, as expected, it was to be nothing. Throughout the remainder of his agony, he lived in the manner of Rodin's *Le Penseur*, his eyes fixed and lacklustre, his body ensconced in an ageless armchair from which he coldly observed his life wilting away – a life that seemed to him to belong to someone else. His only dream now was of a fresh start, somewhere between Papua New Guinea and the Vanuatu Islands. But since this was impossible, he sank into a state of permanent melancholia.

To make matters worse, winter had slowly produced asthmatic symptoms in him. The viscous sound of his breathing turned the stomachs of all his prospective employers. And at the first hoarse cough they would dispense with the most basic empathy and dismiss him at once in disgust, pleading a last-minute meeting or the tyranny of the market. One man even claimed that a fire had just broken out in the first-floor offices. With no friend and no doctor, the ailing man returned home without a word, thinking only of the balm of his wife's embrace on his troubled heart. To be fair, she had vowed to look after him for eternity and, like a nurse, she would run to him, check his pulse, draw him hot baths, prepare broths and suggest a million other ministrations. Knowing that desperate times call for tender measures, she would draw the blinds. And when the room was plunged into this artificial darkness, she would approach to caress the patient – and he would fall asleep in minutes, a smile on his face.

However, our heroine was not a nurse at heart; she was directly descended from three generations of greedy and belligerent women who harboured strange revolutionary fantasies. Her grandmother had run out of patience and flushed her first husband out of the hospital room he thought he'd winter in. Obeying her instincts as a woman of humble origins looking for the first opportunity to climb the social ladder, Madame also had a strong aversion to a down-and-out layabout. Before long she could be heard complaining about her loser of a husband – he was dull, he was lazy, he was sickly.

Six months after they met, in the space of two hollow, rattling breaths, their penniless life eradicated their eternal passion. Mother was the first to complain: cleaning the house was breaking her back, the river water was too cold, the dishes were stacking up in the sink, she didn't get enough sleep. She wanted to be a wife, not a washerwoman. Monsieur was surprised at first – they hardly had any furniture to dust! – but he embraced her and reassured her awkwardly. Millions of women do what you do! Then he came to her aid – he regularly filled the water jug, bought her detergent and a new broom, and even put his dirty cutlery in the sink himself after dinner. But eventually he got angry, told her she was a slacker, threw open the door and left, slamming it shut behind him. His forehead lowered, he went down to the river simmering with rage just like her, determined never to work again. He had been the youngest and in his pampered memories men were born to pass the day in a rocking chair, a handful of cheap peanuts or dates within reach. For everything else, hadn't God created women?

After nine months, even the way one of them chewed meat or how they blinked was enough to seriously irritate the other. As their patience ran thin, they forgot all about the promise of a brand-new world. They wanted to escape. But it was too late; they were married now! Monsieur never forgave himself for his mistake and took refuge under a cloak of silence.

'I was so young, so young!' people would hear him mutter again and again. 'The Dessaintes forced me into this, the scumbags! They tricked me. Did *I* tell you I wanted to marry *you*? You think I ever said that? When? I can't remember. You're lying. I never said it! Your parents put a ring on my finger, just like the hangman puts a head in a noose.'

Mistaking cowardice for pride, he kept a low profile, yet held his head high. How he missed his dear mother! She'd always washed his dirty underwear and satisfied his every whim – even though he'd been a spoiled brat. Constantly complaining that he was tired, he would not get out of bed until late in the afternoon, when crowds of boisterous children had finished school. He would then head straight for the *Comptoir de Chine*, a betting shop and bar where he had discovered a passion for horse-racing.

'They're beautiful, but completely thick, those nags!' he would shout as soon as his wife walked through the sitting room.

To forget that she had married a teenager with developmental issues, she, on the other hand, plunged headfirst into maternity.

'This, at least, will give us a good return!' she would reply to her husband, pointing to her big bare belly.

From the marketplace to the corner shop, from the river to the betting shop where she went looking for my father, she would stroll about as round as a barrel, carrying a tiny resident who was completely unaware of the kind of chaos it would be born into. And, in due course, a child fell from their crooked tree. A son. My brother. Stillborn.

That day, just when a rebirth could have been expected, their life as a couple died a second time. Their Christmas gift was a little clod of cold, dead flesh, its eyes closed and its fists clenched. It moved the nurses on call to tears. Stunned, Father sat on the floor of the delivery room. Head in hands, he mumbled a sentence that no one could understand. But voices could be heard from the corridor: echoes of imminent joy, an impatient woman, a child wanting to live – these sounds were stealing even the first minutes of their eternal mourning. It was the final straw!

Mother came back to rue Descartes, empty-handed and broken-hearted, her belly still swollen from this ghost child. Nothing had changed except in the cemetery, where one small tombstone decorated with chrysanthemums had been added to the rest. For a year, maybe more, not a word could be heard in the Dessaintes household. It was as if the house itself had not survived. They had become a silent couple living in a zombie house. They ate in a hurry, the only sound the clinking of their dishes as they scraped them clean. The rustle of fallen leaves, the creaking of the sheet-metal roof at night, the low hum from the television.

At bedtime Madame took two sleeping pills and immediately fell asleep, face hidden under the sheets. With a bag full of medication within reach and his head propped on his arm, Monsieur would complain about his asthma, the early signs of arthritis, tendonitis in the shoulder, more in his elbow and in his wrist, painful sciatica – and a bleeding ear. If, dozing under the malicious cover of darkness, it so happened that their feet touched, they would spring apart and insult each other furiously. They simply could no longer see past each other's faults.

'This crazy cow wakes up all the time!'

'He snores!'

'She's always tossing and turning!'

'He smells like a horse!'

During the day, Mother would speak of the 'little bastard', and the good gentleman, stirring from his melancholia, would cast doubt on the paternity of the little brat buried in the cemetery. With no one left for the Dessaintes to love, they gave in to their natural inclinations and worshipped their television screen as if it were their longed-for child. It was a match made in heaven: them and the TV. They spent this sad time watching news clips, monsters killing each other and serial murderers dismembering their victims. The only thing they really wanted at this stage – the thing they craved and that sated them – was horror films.

It was in this ghoulish atmosphere that Mother broke the news one morning: she was pregnant again. It was as if a little monster had been created from the brief coupling of one hatred with another. It was my turn to enter their world, two years after a corpse. What did I care if I'd been born out of a misunderstanding, or as some kind of replacement. I had arrived and I intended to stay! But the Dessaintes, who thought otherwise, had put so much effort into hating each other that it was me they ended up loathing.

---

My birth was met with rancour and spite. For nine months, there had been a truce, and the Dessaintes had fought their boredom by trying to find a name. Dorhis, Vladym, Dracchus, Melstrom were my father's favourite serial killers. Why choose one? Their son would have all four, my father decided. On D-Day, he went to place his usual bet on a horse and, as he was near the hospital, he thought that he might go and see his new son. It was the baby's bath time. He slipped into the room and found the child naked. Mother, surprised by this unexpected visit, began to gabble about the baby's beautiful back, their fat calves, plump buttocks, their delicate neck. Bah! He wanted to look at his baby head-on. Mother made a thousand excuses, she chastised him for rushing to the hospital, she asked him how his asthma was. All to no avail. He took the child from her arms and held it up to inspect it. It looked fine to him; he attributed her babbling to the usual silliness of women who have just given birth. Then he discovered what he referred to as the ultimate horror. That thing .... That thing .... That .... It's a girl! It hit him like a thunderclap, and he let go of the child. Of course, his mother had been a girl, as had his grandmother and his wife too – to some extent – but that didn't mean that history should repeat itself. 'Thundering typhoons!' he swore, wiping his arms. A pit bull, fine; a baby giraffe, fine; a three-legged horse or big cockroach, fine ... but a girl! It's like rearing a child who's not right in the head! And all because they had wanted to save twenty francs on an ultrasound! In the end, as an upright man who could not fail to honour his responsibilities, he gave me a crib. But he refused me his name. I spent the next five years screaming at the top of my lungs, preferably at night between three and four in the morning. To be honest, I wasn't crying; I was taking my revenge for my first bath, and using the cast-iron character I'd developed there.

This is where both my story and my downfall began.

———————

How miserable they were, those poor Dessaintes, with a baby girl with a full nappy and a rattle in their sitting room! They'd been expecting a perfect little male with a tyrannical nature and a fighting instinct! In other words, a complete idiot. Instead of him, the heavens had sent them just the sort of relentless, toothless cry-baby that were already thick on the ground in rue Descartes.

After my birth, Mother began to gain weight and Father began to smoke. Father smoked incessantly. But what was particularly unusual was that he never exhaled. The first few nights, as he bent over my crib enveloped in the curls of smoke coming from his cigarette, he wondered if it wouldn't be best to strangle this wrinkly little creature in a babygrow stealing all their sleep. His love of the horses kept growing, as did Mother's thoughts of divorce. But financial dependency, fear of a scandal and serious selfishness made them see sense: a family court judge would mean slipping back into destitution within the hour! A divorce would ruin them both, so there was only one triumphant ending possible: one of them would have to die. But since neither of them was in the mood to kick the bucket, they opted for a fallback solution and turned to the only thing that they still had in common: the money they didn't have. They would raise this disgusting spawn and get some well-deserved financial compensation from the state. It was tacitly agreed between them that they would kick me out of the house as soon as I stopped bringing in money.

A photograph still bears witness to this. I am smiling, looking at the two faces bent over my crib. Father is smiling, thinking about the bets he would be placing over the next eighteen years. My mother is smiling because she was taught to always smile back when people smile at her.

They decided that the best way to get some peace and quiet between fights was to ignore me, just as one pretends to ignore those big house geckos that annoy everyone with their noise and excrement. It was only on days that they were in a very good mood that they bothered to impose their reign of terror on me and use their favourite catchphrase, 'That's the way it is and that's that!'

———————

Like all the other children on rue Descartes, by the time I was four months old I couldn't be weaned from the television. By five months, I had been given my first gift: a poster from one of the Dessaintes' favourite horror films. They put it up on the wall, opposite my bed. Lying on my back in my crib, sucking on the big toe of my left foot, I could be found staring at the strange man, with his awful, torn jumper, his claws instead of fingers. I would soon be affectionately calling him Uncle Fred. He doesn't even have a pom-pom on his funny hat. I gurgle a bit and open my little arms so that he can embrace me, but he stays stoney-faced. I start crying but no one ever comes, so I eventually fall asleep, thinking that this man with his popcorn face must be my dad's brother – they share the same ugly features. At the age of two, I know how to say the important things: 'mum', 'horse', 'betting shop'. I receive two dolls, or *poupettes* as we call them in La Réunion: Bélou and Camille, two sullen little ginger girls. They too are in a very famous horror film that my old man likes to watch. I own two *poupettes* and a poster, and have as much milk as I want, so I more or less behave myself until the age of five. The Dessaintes do not hate me – at least not every day. Living under the same roof creates inescapable bonds: and a child is always useful when it comes to chores. They don't look for jobs because they'd only find one, and that would mean there'd be nobody left to look after me. So they spend the whole day in the sitting room and implore me not to grow up too quickly.

I discover what freedom, cooking and being a mother are all about – they're almost one and the same thing. I spend the morning hours by the river, making mud cakes, pebble buns, a slug fricassee, earthworm spaghetti and gravel jam for my two *poupettes*. In the afternoon, I ask Uncle Fred to look after them while I head out to see the other children in the neighbourhood. I know all of the people who live on rue Descartes: Madame Emelienne, a widow of eighty-three, twice divorced and the owner of a fat cat with the same marital status. She always offers me a yoghurt that is past its use-by date. It's a little sour, but you get used to it. One day, I found maggots wriggling in my raisin pudding. It's a good job I love animals. And a pudding is still a pudding despite the raisins. There's also Jean-José, a confirmed bachelor who acts like a woman every time he gets drunk. A little further down the street, a dozen families – in other words, stay-at-home mums, and dads who go out hunting and fishing – who feast on dishes made up of tiny creatures like young gobies, dried shrimps, wasp larvae and coquilles. Each couple has four or five children, all barefoot, all armed with a sling for taking out birds, lizards and starfruits. I am the youngest, so I always remain a little apart. I leave one house to go to another, am passed from one person to their neighbour, from one side of the street to the other; and I come back at night without anyone noticing that I had been gone all day.

But at the age of six, I begin to turn bad, as the Dessaintes like to say. The telly and the neighbourhood are no longer enough for me. I am afflicted with an ailment that is common to all ill-loved children: a hysterical craving for parental attention. So I stick to them like glue. I recite the alphabet at the top of my voice; count up to fifty, fifty times in a row; tirelessly recite the same poem, 'For you, Mummy, Lovely Mummy'; go away and hide for five seconds, only to come straight back; jump on the sofa in the sitting room until I am out of breath; endlessly imitate the sound of the neighbour's cat or rooster – swearing it wasn't me. I also make my bed, clean the yard and never belch. All in vain! The Dessaintes always respond to my energy and vigour with a sigh or a shake of the head, or they just turn up the volume on the TV. Focused, silent, immobile, Father stares at the screen, his chin resting on his fist. He is deaf to my sighs, to my dances, to all my sorrowful laments.

'In that film yesterday, all the little boys were so well behaved!' he says.

In utter desperation, next I go for one of those nursery rhymes that are so cute they would melt the most icy heart, and I start singing the irresistible 'Mitty Matty Had a Hen', which my relentless parents finish up with 'She laid eggs only for villains'.

I don't know why what followed happened, but it did. I don't know why I didn't just keep my mouth shut. I'm still asking myself whether it should and could have been avoided.

'Our teacher says that people who watch TV all day long like you are idiots who will never accomplish anything in their lives. And that's that!'

The serenity of the Dessaintes lay in splinters, as did the wooden door of the sitting room. They charged down from the heavens. With the universe as their witness, they bellowed in one voice, in a single raging blast:

'How dare you?! You think you're better than us? You think you'll do any better? You'll never, ever see any further than the end of your own nose! From now on, you can take care of yourself, on your own, all alone, and we'll be keeping score! We'll see what's what, when it comes down to it.'

For weeks on end, the Dessaintes, whose hatred is extremely tenacious, had faces a hundred feet long. At best, they bellowed in unison once more: 'Your own nose! No further than your own nose!' At worst, they ignored me completely.

My perverse nature forced me into an occupation that would keep me entertained for the many years to come: proving to the Dessaintes that they were wrong – that I could see further than my olfactive protuberance, that I could do better than them, in every way possible. From then on, the die was cast: my life was a game of Snakes and Ladders ruled by my parents' hatred and my obsession with revenge. At least, that's what Mistress Bélina, my school teacher, said, going on the stories I fed her during break. According to the Dessaintes' version, it was as simple as this: 'She's nuts, this maggot, and she's getting on our nerves.' Spurred by a fever of precocious rage – a thorn in their side – I'd always get back in the saddle, as my father would have put it. War had been declared! And I was intent on winning it.

To prevent their children going to school, parents on rue Descartes come up with the best of ploys: they willingly write excuse notes and keep doing so until the last year of secondary school – if anyone ever gets that far.

'Don't go to school if you don't feel like it,' said my dad whenever he opened his mouth. 'It's pointless anyway.'

Which is why I began to go twice as much. I woke up much earlier than I needed to and announced that I hated the holidays as loudly as I could just to annoy him.

Impatient every morning, I waited for the neighbourhood gang of Black and mixed-race children at the corner of the street. They looked like orphans: their eyes still shiny with sleep, hair tangled, feet trapped in beige plastic sandals. Like ants around a discarded lollipop, they swarmed the bus stop from all sides. Humming, we stomped around and swapped marbles and cards until a woman from the neighbourhood – no matter who – arrived. She was immediately designated the leader of our party; she would take us to Girofles School on the other side of the river. In the midst of this abominable, this joyful crowd – which moved to the warm, thudding rhythm of children tripping each other up and playing spontaneous hopscotch – I began to imagine how I could 'do better'. This phrase haunted me for a reason I didn't quite understand. I was the child who spoke the most, ate the most biscuits, ran the fastest and also got on people's nerves the most. In school, my heart beating in a frenzy of revenge, I recited the alphabet, studied arithmetic, learned poetry, practised drawing. But when evening came, nobody ever asked me what I studied, heard or remembered.

As for what the Dessaintes were doing in my absence, I had no idea; I never missed a single day of school anymore. I imagine that Mother, between rounds of insults aimed at her best enemy, cleaned the house, put rice on to boil, prepared a *carri* and washed our clothes. Father, for his part, would try to fix a stool, put up a shelf or mend a rickety henhouse while working on his retorts. His nickname, 'All-thumbs Dessaintes', must have been the result of one such masterpiece. All I deduced when I returned home from school, thanks to the shards of broken glass or bits of plate, was that the Dessaintes still hadn't mastered the art of juggling. That inspired me! Two weeks later, I had already mastered juggling with two small balls. School replaced my parents and taught me everything I needed to know about life.

The best memory I have of primary school dates back to my third year. Our teacher had slipped a small illustrated book into each of our bags. I brought it back to rue Descartes and was planning on starting it that evening while my parents were watching TV. Night had fallen some time before, the punctual crowing of an insomniac rooster marking the hour. Twenty past midnight. The door of the sitting room opened slightly, and a little head with a peculiar bun on top threw a worried glance into the darkness. That was me. Father had gone out earlier, and he still hadn't come back home!

When those who live in the great Babels of Europe or Asia picture nights on a tropical island, they see a long desert draped in peaceful dreams. A secret Thebaid scene. A refuge draped in black velvet until the next sunrise. This might be true for the Kerguelen Islands, Adélie Land and New Amsterdam, where the eternal winter has frozen all thirst for adventure and bestial aggression. But here, in the heat of the Tropic of Capricorn, on the flanks of an active volcano, the sharks would even tear apart your favourite magazine if only they could crawl as far as your beach towel and the nights are a constant circus. Quiet times and places are rare.

At seven in the evening, in the high grass, under the croton hedges, on mounds of white gravel – in other words, everywhere – a recital by invisible cicadas accompanies the double concerto for pots and pans that has attracted a famished audience to the dining room. At eight, depending on the film that evening, muskets, machine guns or pipe bombs reverberate in the sitting room. From nine onwards, it's time for the neighbourhood dogs to call out to each other from courtyard to courtyard. The incessant barking only ceases when a neighbour fires a gun, aiming, one hopes, at the sky. Let there be silence! But only until eleven – a twenty-minute respite! For eleven marks the start of the illegal racing of cars and motorbikes, known as *pousses* or *rodeos*. It's loud enough to leave you deaf and can wake the soundest of sleepers – everyone, that is, apart from the local law enforcement officers. As soon as the roaring engines stop, the bin men start their rounds with a small dustcart, and that racket can be heard all the way to Saint-Joseph. Right under your window, you can hear the sound of glass being smashed, your car being scratched and bins being banged about. Scarcely have the bin men entered the next street when the street cats slink on stage! Each feline, so phlegmatic and distinguished during the day, starts meowing insult after insult, runs around like mad, yowls like a prowling cheetah and challenges all those eyeing its territory with a phosphorescent, dilated stare. Then the melée! Hysterical furballs with their claws out, threatening growls, plaintive cries – a clash on the tin roof overhead, a crash against the grill of a rabbit hutch. The hens panic, the cock (barely recovered from last night's fight) crows at the top of his lungs, and the baby wakes up and starts bawling for its bottle. And then, suddenly, nothing. It is four in the morning and, with the first signs of dawn, the thunderous battalions abandon the front line, promising to meet again that very evening. Nights on Bourbon (as the kings used to call it) know little peace and the Reunionese sleep only in snatches.

I wasn't bothered by any of the noise; it was just strange that my father was still out there, far from home. To kill time, I grabbed the first book that came to hand; it was something our school teacher had lent us. I sank, stupefied, into a parallel universe, a world different from the one they kept ramming down my throat at home. Both places were strange alright, but the one in the little book was much more welcoming. From bandits like Sitarane and Saint-Ange, I moved onto Uncle Belo, a good-natured old blue cat, whose walking stick, glasses and Father Christmas beard immediately inspired feelings of warmth and trust. The old man, forever clad in his gardening overalls, seemed to have an emotional interest in his grandchildren's education, as well as that of their friend, a green rat. After hearing my fair share of local folktales, from the footless dancer of the nightclubs in the West through to Lom-Kok's chuckles and the needle swallowers in the Hindu temple, I wasn't about to be scared by a simple green rat – no doubt gnawing on a chayote leaf. He wasn't much to write home about given the freaks I was used to on rue Descartes. To be honest, I couldn't even read at that stage, but I contented myself with the pictures, and got a huge amount out of them. The entire Chaudron zoo paraded before my eyes: the depressed elephants, the impassive kangaroo, the morose ostriches and even the sleepy wildcats. But I'd hardly had time to look at it all before I heard the key turn in the lock: Father was back. He did not take the book from my hands; nor did he even notice it. Mother came in – I don't know what was eating her – and she ignored me as well.

A few weeks later, when I returned home, I found her busy in the kitchen. Father was fixing the television. I grabbed the little book out of my school bag and opened it up. A group of jumbled black arabesques was dancing on a little white wall – an entire world of words and meanings that completely escaped me. I tried to capture one or two, but they were too stubborn, too resilient. So, I hurried off to present them to Mother, placing my index finger under those unknown formulas. Without stopping her work, she bent over and indifferently pronounced the words that were causing me so much trouble. That was what they meant! *Holidays.* Secretly I was very much looking forward to them. *School.* I had just come back from there. *Circus.* Where I lived. I marvelled at this cascade of meaning and at the ease with which Mother – covered in soapsuds up to her elbows and her head festooned with curlers – managed to lift the mysterious veil surrounding each group of letters. She deciphered them all in triumph. Tired of resisting, each one admitted defeat and obediently joined the line of well-behaved and neatly arranged words in the vanquished paragraph. I was overjoyed. I bore no grudge, I immediately forgot their imperious silence: I worshipped them as sacred beings.

'*During the holidays, Ratus, Marou and Mina go to circus school.*' Good Lord! I almost know how to read!

'*Ratus, Marou and Mina go to circus school.*' Alleluia!

Ten minutes later, I was still admiring the perfection of this sentence. Then came the next one. I understood it all on my own and read it aloud:

' *"Easy!" said Ratus, chewing on his cheese.*'

I was speechless. Quick! Someone give me the name of the genius who invented writing – and such a line! I had to meet him and offer him some nougatine and sesame balls!

*'Easy!' said Ratus, chewing on his cheese?* So Ratus spoke with his mouth full too. Full of cheese and confidence. Full of words and certainty. From then on, I demanded that the Dessaintes call me Ratus, much to their dismay! And I began to regularly commit a crime that neither of them would have dreamt of: I read! Worse still, I enjoyed it! Thoroughly. So thoroughly that I worked out how to beat those scoundrels: I would read, and invent stories, and make my own books. I would rise above my station and go places people couldn't imagine me in. Mistress Bélina used to sing out: *'Alta alatis patent!'* But it was just teacher's jargon to me. In my head, a vigorous 'Attack!' resounded, and, at the age of seven, I set about launching one for real.

I decided to become a writer (at the time I didn't know they were all suicidal, neurotic, alcoholic megalomaniacs). I would become a writer and recount the further adventures of the animals of Le Chaudron. I would become a writer and create magic – and this would infuriate my parents, those TV devotees. I was ready to rebel: there was just one obstacle left to overcome. I would need to learn to write. With this objective in mind, I went to school every day, and spent the rest of the time devouring books in the school library. But not once did I consider asking my parents for any. Used to their absence at home, I believed that only school had the right to own them. Until I started secondary school, I was unaware that the world boasts shops dedicated exclusively to the sale of books – and even has libraries rash enough to lend them out free of charge. To be completely honest we did have one book at home – a dictionary – but it was used only to hold the door open. I thought it had been designed for that purpose. Even among the eccentric gifts they received on their wedding night, the Dessaintes did not find a single book. Not even a cookbook.

From then on, I would barely be home from school before I'd install Camille and Bélou at my feet and read – or rather stammer out – stories of blue hills and Eden-like valleys where rivers of hot chocolate flow. Soon, carried away by my shameless obsession, I read absolutely anything that I could find: the advertisements piled up in the sitting room, the television guide, bills to pay, the leaflet that came with Madame Dessaintes' anti-depressants. But I didn't read quietly. I shouted out almost every word. It was essential that the Dessaintes heard me reading. Until they came at me with the belt – which always happened in the end – I read at a volume guaranteed to make me lose my voice. In the meantime, the Dessaintes set a new plan in motion. First, I found it astonishing that Ratus *falls from the flower while putting up the rainbow*. Then I discovered that life was just a sequence of oddities: why else would page twenty come immediately after page seventeen. Finally, I understood that the Dessaintes were pulling out every other page. To try to make some sense of these underhand acts, I set off for school to explain it all to Mistress Bélina, she who is sure to understand, to explain, and to resolve everything.

———————

Mistress Bélina had just announced to her dear pupils that Father Christmas had arrived from Lapland. Each child would be photographed with the white-haired old man except the most unruly young boys who, she had warned, would have to content themselves with the reindeer. The battle that I was fighting against those titans – my parents – and their scowls suddenly became less pressing. My main concern that day was to find favour in the eyes of my favourite Lapp. Dressed in sapphire blue, my heart pounding, I went to meet Father Christmas at eleven o'clock. He had arrived before all the children and was seated on a white rattan chair in the middle of the school garden. There was an enormous sack at his feet, overflowing with presents. Light-hearted with glee, we hovered around the old man in a fever of anticipation. Mistress Bélina had been detained somewhere or other, so we children larked about with increasing energy, jumping around one bush, into another, under a third – always reappearing, as if by chance, in Santa's line of sight. When it was my turn to be photographed with him, I approached with rapid steps, trembling. I was about to experience the very best moment of my year – but it turned out to be the most unsettling.

Infantile hysteria is one thing, disappointment another, but when the two coincide it's utterly perturbing. Imagine Mistress Bélina, who had the whole nursery school believe she owned a cat, went to bed at eight o'clock every evening and dedicated her Sundays to accordion dances, flowery dresses and white dahlias … Mistress Bélina, who claimed to live in a semidetached house in the suburb of Cité Labourdonnais …. Mistress Bélina, who had a daughter, was herself a daughter, and who only ever wore women's clothes … Imagine Mistress Bélina is none other than Father Christmas!

I should have known! Particularly given her deep voice, thick body hair and hairy cheeks! I said nothing to my classmates, but this discovery dumbfounded me for the rest of the day. What was the point in old Bélina concealing the truth, having us call her mistress every day, wearing that grotesque layer of make-up? She could have just confessed to us all at the start that she was the queen of Lapland. Adults are certainly very difficult to understand. That afternoon, I went home with two photos. In one, which shows my unbridled joy, you could see a huge smile, a pair of little eyes gazing tenderly at the god of presents. In the other, taken a second later: two enormous wide eyes black with confusion, shoulders caught in a shudder, shaggy little plaits, and a thin index finger pointing towards the androgynous old coot who, between *ségas*, had secretly grazed Dasher and Prancer under Lapland's snowy firs. I couldn't resist stopping beneath the sitting room window and looking once again at the portrait of that ridiculous old person with painted nails.

In that moment, something in my head shatters. I feel as if my body, all my energy, my entire being is a sheet of paper being slowly torn up. I experience a sense of absolute tragedy that exceeds my childish understanding. They've lied to me? They've lied to us all! Is it possible for something other than the truth to exist? For Father Christmas to be a woman? Or for him not to exist? Is it even possible for adults to lie? Is it allowed? Does it happen often? From my eyes falls something like a butterfly's tear. Looking all about me, I try to locate some reason for this huge betrayal. I am nauseous, disillusioned, drunk with disgust. I now understand that adults prefer lies to children's happiness. There's simple sincerity in 'no, he doesn't exist', but they prefer to indulge in barbarisms.

And then, before I had any time to recover from this umpteenth deception, I was passing by a window at home and overheard my parents – who were conducting a momentary truce – having a conversation.

They had taken the joint decision to move on to the next stage. The one thing they agreed on was that their good-for-nothing, despotic brat was beginning to wear them out. For all the trouble I'd caused – the nose business as they so neatly put it – the only just remedy was Apeca. Apeca: a pretentious acronym that referred to an association for juvenile delinquents and abandoned children, an expression that was in itself both pointlessly long and deceptive. It denoted hell for all badly brought-up children. In other words: the house of correction! As usual, Father said nothing, but his silence spoke of only his tacit approval. The news hit me like a cannon ball. I listened even harder, hoping it was a misunderstanding, but my mother repeated the name twice more. Apeca! Apeca! They had done everything they could, tried everything possible, but now it was a matter for the benevolent hands of the experts in a reformatory high up on La Plaine des Cafres. I staggered drunkenly towards the river, overcome, my joy shattered to pieces. First my nose, then Father Christmas, now the house of correction! Behind me, the daily avalanche of my parents' grievances and complaints swept down with even more ferocity than usual. Each one blamed the other for the birth of this unwanted child; they raised their hands to the heavens declaring to anyone who cared to listen that they had nothing to reproach themselves for.

To me it felt as if the whole garden had learnt the news: a bee, witnessing the dispute, flew in a panic and spread the story from root to creeper, bush to petal, bud to rock. The result was that, when I reached the river, the entire universe appeared to scream my sentence. 'The house of correction! Apeca! The house of correction! Oh, and by the way, Father Christmas is Mistress Bélina.'

Apeca. Good grief! That place with narrow, bricked-up windows, where half of the staff were humourless tyrants and the other half were devils who licked children into shape with a whip and a hot poker. What would become of me in this Gehenna where the most recalcitrant children were left to be eaten by their comrades? How would I survive there, even for a day? Would Father Bélina at least deliver presents there? I confess that I wept. I lashed out at this terrible vision, which had, on this occasion, taken on the form of my pink schoolbag. Finally tiring of attacking an invincible adversary, and thoroughly disgusted with myself, I climbed to the top of the bank with an aching wrist and watched the river swirling below. The shudder that passed from the branches to the surface of the water ceaselessly whispered: 'House of correction, Father Christmas doesn't exist, house of correction, Father Bélina is Mother Christmas, house of correction.'

The rocks were squirrel grey: the same shade as the doors of the house of correction. A dreadful premonition caught me. Where would I find the courage to live? Thus, at the age of eight, I resolved to end it all. Dying was the only viable solution. I would drown myself in the whirlpool at my feet. But, as the indifferent day spent its final rays on this suicidal scene, a sturdy hand grabbed me by the collar and I was treated to a severe hiding. Which made two in less than forty-eight hours, above average for the Dessaintes.

In light of the circumstances, I postponed my attempt until a more favourable time and ran back inside. 'When will you stop persecuting your poor parents?' Mother grumbled. And a slap from the belt and two kicks in my back suggested I stop that very minute. A plate of pancakes was placed on the kitchen table that evening. You take your consolation where you can.

---

All the evidence suggested that my campaign of incessant complaint had gone as far as it could. Happily, Camille and Bélou had remained on the right side, and the enemy hadn't thought of taking them hostage. In war, anything is possible after all.

We meet for a council, them lying down facing the sky, me distractedly scratching in the dust the drawbridge and portcullis that would soon lead me to certain hell. We decide to radically change our approach. We bravely agree on immediate and complete concession, accompanied by a systematic yes to everything the Dessaintes might ask from me. Our family will take on a new configuration. On the one hand, there will be my pitiful parents; on the other, the new me, willing and obsequious, obedient and unassuming. No sooner said than done! From then on, I wash the car on my own and unblock the sink in the kitchen and the handbasin in the bathroom without asking for help. And I keep score: two months with no house of correction! I learn to cook for three, I leave the best space on the couch for my father and always allow him to speak first. I win five more months. I no longer forget to wake him or to make his bed before getting ready for school. Apeca is now one year ago, but it remains on everybody's lips.

And, alas, the interminable evenings in the company of the Dessaintes offer endless opportunities for a faux pas. First you have to endure without complaint a meal that even the English wouldn't envy (probably the reason they were so rare on the island at the time). Always rice. Always white. Only white was allowed back then on rue Descartes. With it, cassoulet, corned beef, chicken drumsticks or, worst of all, pilchards in tomato sauce: that large, cheap depressive sardine that splashes about in the Channel between Dover and Calais. Its taste varies between very bad and revolting. But I no longer retch with disgust: I gobble it up without a single grimace.

The meal over, my parents position themselves in the sitting room, wrapped in wreaths of white smoke from my father's cigarettes, again lying forgotten on the side of the ashtray. When we are all ready, I seize the remote control. Out of the peaceful obscurity surge a thousand beams of light: a thousand rainbows of garish and infernal colour are reflected in the mute grey windows of our veranda. It's time for the start of the show, starring, every evening, the dregs of humanity. Monsters! Acts of treachery! Vendettas!

Shush! The Dessaintes are watching television.

For hours, abominable displays of torture would follow: infamous scenes of amputations – tongues, ears and breasts torn off. Knees smashed with a hammer, elbows sliced with a billhook, blood spouting from savagely cut throats, nails driven into the victims' stupefied eyes. Or fingernails removed with a knife, frail hands forced into a burning-hot toaster, whole arms fed through a crusher. Or shootings at point-blank range, skulls blown to pieces – the smouldering pink pulp of the ruined brain spurting out. A flagellated back turns blue, splits open, splintering into a profusion of blood and broken bone. Wedged into an armchair as if hypnotized – open-mouthed and heart frozen – I watch this summation of untold bestiality that fascinates my parents so much. On the table, the coffee goes cold. In the bathroom, water drips endlessly into the basin. It is on the point of overflowing. A fly has been desperately tapping against the glass for an hour. The world has gone deaf, paralysed by horror on a sagging couch.

Often, my swamped mind unable to take any more, darkness would draw over my eyes like a thick curtain. The murder scenes, the barbaric acts, the unbearable coitus, the sliced or swollen flesh: everything blurred together under the anaesthetic influence of sleep or a fainting fit. But even though those monsters and their martyrs were gone, their cries crept along the blackout curtains, looking for a chink, a passage however narrow to creep through and allow them to tear me gently from the peace of night. I tried putting my hands over my ears. I pretended not to hear anything, to still be sleeping. Impossible. The horrors on show were always succeeded by a ceaseless string of heartrending distraught entreaties, bestial grunts, slaps and shouts. 'Die! Die! Kill him! Kill!'

Sometimes there were strange noises. They were impossible to identify amidst the flapping wings and sobbing children. They sounded like rutting cries, the orgies of centaurs; groans from women, sometimes outraged, sometimes impassioned, but always at the mercy of men, men by the dozen who hit them, who whipped them, who called them the most obscene of names. At other times, there were murmurs of joy or indignation, or awful, dry groans that spoke of suffering and the fear of death.

I opened my eyes. Regretfully. My heart was beating, fit to burst, in a land where man was a delirious wildcat, drunk on rage, debauchery and cruelty. The beads of sweat – of terror and outrage – on my forehead were the same as those of the victims. I watched, eyelids lowered, heard the cries. Never-ending horrors seemed to pass before my eyes, even when they were closed. I was no longer watching them. I was living them. Seated on the couch of a nameless planet lit by three suns, powerless and on edge, I leapt as if in a dream. I fled monsters and armies, I hurtled down slopes, I called for a sword. Despite the dark, I had to press on, I had to find my way out of this infernal jungle. The scene changed.

A moonless night. I switched on a light: my parents grumbled. I turned it off straightaway and resolved to turn back, alone, into the thick darkness. In front of me, without me knowing, an awful creature was also advancing. An indomitable behemoth, looking for me to take me to Apeca. Silence. A key fell. I was lost. I felt the shadow of a smooth and icy hand seize my shoulder.

'No!' I shouted as loud as I could.

This long and desperate cry roused my parents from their slumber. They stood up. I, as usual, had collapsed.

'What are you doing? Go and sleep in your bed! Otherwise, it's the reformatory tomorrow morning. And that's that.'

Frantic, I stood up, still aching from imaginary blows, my pyjamas dripping wet from terror. Eventually assured that my heart was not going to give out, I groped my way along to my little pink bed. I have been stripped of my innocence, but I am alive and still free. Force-fed a diet of unspeakable things and deprived of sleep, but I am alive and still free. I have the right number of arms and legs; nothing has been cut off. So I head off to sleep. After all, I know there is worse elsewhere: that is to say, at La Plaine des Cafres.

―――――――――

During one of these nights of carnage, an unknown feeling began to form in me, one whose very name – associated as it was in my mind with crudeness and sublime villainy – thwarted the love that I had for my parents. From then on, it held sway by day as well as by night, persisting, swelling and inflating to such an extent that it began to take terrific efforts to try and erase its impression. Yes, it was at this time that I began to be ashamed of my parents.

Ashamed of their indifference, of their tendency to treat me as an adult. Ashamed of their ability to excuse themselves from all constraint, to not answer to any sense of conscience. Ashamed of their utter lack of remorse, the absence of any scruples. Something fearful emerged from the labyrinth of my child's mind. Something that going to school, and seeing other fathers and mothers, made more and more obvious. My parents were not normal people. They were from a separate race that dwelled at the very bottom of the cesspool. I didn't hate them; I pitied them.

At the age of nine, without really knowing why, I stopped watching horror films. But this longed-for respite brought me even greater angst. I could still hear, every evening, cries of rage, brutish roaring and sustained artillery attacks. Though I wasn't able to see it, the sounds alone were enough to send you mad. The endless clangour woke terrors that had been slumbering in my mind. Accustomed to abnormal levels of depravation already, I was prompted to more obscene imaginings – things more monstrous and more bloody than even I was familiar with. Each thump reverberated in my ribs; each rattle of the guns drove an ice axe into my skull. At around three in the morning, overcome by the chorus of shouts, gunfire, entreaties and profanity, remembering that there was school the next day, I rose noiselessly and entered the sitting room. Mother was asleep; I turned off the television and placed a blanket over her. Another day with the Dessaintes had drawn to a close. Another day far from the house of correction. It was something. The worst was still some distance away.

———————

The worst is the end of the world, and it came all the same. One week in October when I was nine years old. In the silver twilight, gnawed by the heat of the night. There was no fanfare. No warning signs. Just a dark sky scattered into a thousand fragments. A minute before, my ninth summer had been going splendidly – that's to say it was bearable. A minute before, the scent of the allamandas and the frangipani were flooding into our sitting room. Bélou was with me and my parents. We had finished a walk and returned home, all four of us. It seems there was one word, one exasperation too many. Suddenly, in my hair, at my feet, there were only fragments of that orangey world. It had been lost forever. A chair, still warm, was pushed away in terror. Then a second. A monster as big as a tornado was rolling towards us. In the stunned shadows, I clutched Bélou tight and tried to hide behind an armchair, a cupboard, the fan – anything at all. Bélou was very scared. Her heart was pounding against mine. She began to tremble and started to cry. I wanted to reassure her, but I couldn't find the words.

'Stop it, Bélou,' I said. 'Stop it. It's nothing. We just have to stay hidden.'

But Bélou was too small to understand adult matters. All she could do was cry. She didn't know how to avert her eyes, the way Mistress Bélina taught us to at school.

Things were falling on our heads, hitting our shoulders, our hands. I held Bélou to me and we ran to hide behind the kitchen door. But on the threshold we stopped dead, shocked by the peacefulness of the outside world.

Within, the Dessaintes, mired in their hatred, were having a go at gladiatorial combat. They had come to blows – kicking and slapping one another, dragging each other by the hair through the middle of the sitting room.

Now that I come to think of it, perhaps there had been a rumbling or some small murmur to presage this event after a day of rain. But neither Bélou nor I expected the world to end then, in that cool, blue-grey dusk. I would certainly have preferred the apocalypse – the real one – to this commotion, to this loss of innocence. It left me an orphan even though my parents were still there. Because at 21 rue René-Descartes, a cast-iron pot had whirled its way through the air, and now the two Dessaintes were hitting each other in determined silence, their tense, sweaty bodies knotted into a fight to the death. All over one word too many.

One of them was lying on the ground. The other was spitting blood. And yet there was no prospect of a truce. One of the two had to die: night had to fall on a corpse. There was no reason to spare Bélou's feelings. She had to learn to live with this. No crying, not a single tear! Await the end of the war. So despite my disgust and exhaustion, despite the night outside, I wrapped Bélou in a woollen blanket and we fled. We went looking for a diplomat, a personification of peace – anything, anyone, anywhere – to come and save us, or at least what remained of us.

I ran at top speed along the street. It felt immense as a city, black and threatening with its barking wolves, its high-pitched swallows forming strange circles below the clouds. I moved quickly, as if I was in a dream. As if I was in a film. Braving the packs of dogs wandering without a master. Seeking a single soul but finding only shut-up houses, chained gates, huge hounds ready to bite. Bélou won't stop asking if they're both dead, like on TV. In the distance, a shadow makes her jump. It's nothing, Bélou. It's nothing. I turn back and then – out of breath, in a different place – cross the road audaciously, swept along by a golden spotlight. A car goes past.

Enormous. Roaring like a beast. The mark of tyres brought to a brutal halt can still be seen on the ground several weeks later. It hasn't killed us. No chance! I refuse to die today.

We have already disappeared into the courtyard of a building. We stay there, crouched down, panting. In the midst of this explosion of fear, Bélou continues asking if they are both dead. I stand up and resume my journey, but this time I know where to go: to the Bertrands, a family from Champagne who have lived in the next street for the past year. They have a fat ginger cat, a swing and three children. Monsieur Bertrand owns a small moped-repair shop; his wife works in an office. I'm sure they'll know what to do. I push open the gate, cross their garden and abruptly open the door to the house – they never lock it. All five of them are seated in the huge sitting room, bathed in light. Next to them, Paul-Émile, their Persian cat, is absent-mindedly following their discussion while watching the televised repeat of a ballet.

'Please, come quickly. My parents are fighting!'

The man and woman stood up immediately. This spontaneity acted like a balm on my humiliated heart. They believed me straightaway! Straightaway. They trusted me! I forgot that I had arrived at their house with bare feet and a crying doll. How could they not have believed me? In any case, simply crossing the road was enough to reveal those two dark, pitiless masses for what they were, each devoid of any honour and living only to slit the other's throat. Madame Bertrand held me in her arms while I held Bélou in mine. She and her husband ran across the road. Neither my father nor my mother saw us arrive. The room reverberated with insults and kicks. They had no time to lose. Harm had to be done! Stab. Wear down. Strangle. Belittle. In the flurry of the fight, their hands sought anything – a vase, lamp, frying pan – that might deliver the coup de grâce. One of them had just landed on their salvation. There was a glimpse of a fist holding a knife, piercing the night as it plunged into battle.

'That's enough!' yelled Monsieur Bertrand. 'That's enough!'

But their combat had rendered them impervious to the world around them. They lived only to strike, ready to bleed to death as long as they ultimately vanquished their foe. Monsieur Bertrand did the only thing that was still possible: he took a deep breath and plunged his warm, bear-like body into the frenzy of heaving, panic-stricken flesh. After what felt like an infinity, he managed to pull them apart. The three bodies collapsed like the columns of a temple that had been laid to waste. As if pulled from a nightmare, all three shook their confused heads and started to look around in astonishment. It was like the day after the end of the world, when each survivor, paying little attention to the others, first contemplates the damage done to the ruined earth, marvelling at their survival. Is it really me? Is the world still turning?

Those Dessaintes! What performers! And to think it was me they wanted to send to the house of correction!

They stood up, ashamed and downcast. Their sharp teeth were concealed in their crimson mouths, their claws had become hands again, and each trickle of blood that slid down their cheeks was now elongated by a tear of disgust and a sigh of regret. Regret at not having been the sole survivor.

Bélou and I slipped from Madame Bertrand's arms and went to stand between these stunned Goliaths. After all, in wartime, peace is the only thing that counts. After reassuring them both, Monsieur Bertrand took to lecturing them.

My parents detested me even more after that: I had revealed what went on behind closed doors. Hatred, hunger and blows as savage as the breakers of the Sud Sauvage were acceptable, but it was essential to keep up appearances. How others see you, the external signs of success, the flashy car – all these were sacred under the Tropic of Capricorn.

The cacophony of their hatred could be heard that night even from the other side of town. Let's say it was the pinnacle of their wretchedness. But in terms of the neighbourhood as a whole, it was nothing new. Between ourselves, all couples threw the kitchen sink at one another several times a year on rue Descartes. A little bust-up or *ralé-poussé* as they put it. What is strange is that while everyone knew, and everyone did the same thing, denying all evidence with a flood of refutations was a point of honour. No doubt a twisted spirit lingered here.

One thing is certain: the following day, along the canal where people fished for gobies, at the betting shop and bar, in the queue at the post office, it was all anyone talked about. The Dessaintes were trying their hand at Thai boxing too! Money from eleven-year-old bets changed hands. People recalled the predictions on the evening of the marriage, congratulated themselves as oracles, swore they had seen it all coming. It had happened: the Dessaintes were finished.

Though not quite. They had a daughter determined to succeed, someone who paid scrupulous attention to her own future and therefore vague attention to theirs as the two were sadly linked.

———————

At this stage, I had the good idea of teaming up with the daughter of one of our new neighbours. As a present for my ninth birthday, she gave me her personal copy of the Gospels and a glass of grenadine. As I had read and reread my supply of books, I was consumed with passion for this ream of thin paper and fervently recited this passionate defence of the poor in spirit, the famished and the persecuted Palestinians. You might think it had been written for the Dessaintes and me. I could never have imagined the reaction of my parents when they heard the ascent to Calvary. Although I didn't understand three quarters of what I was reading, they experienced a supreme revelation. It was the perfect new gobbledygook to relieve the flatness of their existence. Before I had had time to finish the book, they had rustled up two enormous and mysterious bibles from God knows where. Sometimes they used them as armrests, sometimes as a hobby. And, not content with drinking from the great cup of sacred words on their own, they began studying the New Testament every week with a couple of Holy Joes.

For some years, the poorest neighbourhoods had been swarming with these tie-wearing missionaries. They waylaid underage mothers, the unemployed and others in need of a crutch, spouting verses that announced either the advent of paradise or the imminence of the world's end, depending on their mood at the time and the degree of sympathy that their audience inspired in them. Their victims, struck dumb through incomprehension, were rarely hostile. So one Saturday morning, a pair of these believers appeared at our gate, a bible under one arm and a child in the other. While those around the Dessaintes considered them to be a couple of nobodies governed by the whims of social services – though they didn't say it aloud as they were in the same boat themselves – these people had come to prove, with the support of a chapter of the Gospels, that a god existed who was foolhardy and thoughtless enough to love them, to ascribe them some value and to pardon all their faults. Moreover, said god seemed to be very partial to large-scale massacres – to the point of contemplating committing an umpteenth one very shortly. Needless to say, my two great lovers of apocalyptic films plunged headlong into these spectacular stories and read them with the same joyful solemnity that they put into reading the week's major short news items. The good old scraps and machete blows onscreen were now supplemented by the biblical promise of imminent seraphic combat with swords, hailstone showers, fireballs and horsemen straight out of outer space. To tell the truth, all this came at an opportune moment. For some time, the horror that played out in full each evening in the sitting room had taken on a liturgical tone of such predictability that the two Dessaintes had been stricken with boredom. Now their dreams were peopled by new stories, just as bloody but brand new.

After a few weeks, the Dessaintes would descend into raptures over any religious impulse or trinket – a rosary, a hymn, a wooden crucifix, a phial of holy water. Just as you or I might descend into drink or ruin. They would also slide into a trance. On Saturday afternoon, for example, shortly before the repeat of the Muppet Show. Not one after the other, but at the same time. Father, with a Christlike air – rings hollowed around his eyes so they looked like oysters, his cheeks sunken, his palms lifted to the sky – positioned himself under an avocado tree and, speaking nothing but Aramaic, preached repentance, the kingdom of God and the Beatitudes to a congregation of maggots, panther chameleons and different cardinal birds. Mother – mystical, fervent, passionate – ran back and forth, screamed like a wild boar with its throat cut and flung herself prostrate in our sweet potato patch. The neighbours watched through the fence as these two incorrigible nutters put on their usual variety show. I was no longer appalled and didn't pay them any attention. I knew that at precisely 5:17 p.m. it would all finish as it had begun: in one of those unspeakable rows. Believing it to be the True Cross, one of them would try to climb the electricity pole. Then, I would have to stop doing my chores – the dishes, the housework or the laundry – for a few minutes. Then, like the Saturday before and the Saturday to come, I would have to call the fire brigade, the electricity company and the priest. Then, someone would try to put straitjackets on them and the Dessaintes would scream. *Noli me tangere, Satana.* Saturdays were a carnival: lots of coloured lights, plenty of strangers dressed up in costume.

As I wait and I endure, still resolved to fight on all fronts to avoid the reformatory, I become a brilliant student, a remarkable housekeeper and a terrific apostle all at the same time. Bring on John's Apocalypse, the Sermon on the Mount and the Epistles to the Corinthians. I am able to read so I devour three chapters of the Bible each day. I like singing so I hum an *Ave Maria* under my cold shower. I have some salt dough left so I make little crucifixes and Wailing Walls.

During the holidays, which the Dessaintes spend together, each keeping to themselves, I split myself in two as best I can. Come with mummy, she'll get you an ice cream this morning! Follow me, my little girl, how about a pony ride this afternoon? It's party time! I get two tamarind sorbets in the same day, two lemonades and two walks to the park. But two beatings as well.

Once night fell I could boast of a unique privilege. The sole of her left foot positioned like a screen before my eyes, I was allowed to scrape away at Madame Dessaintes' toes while she told me, for the umpteenth time, about how Yael, with a simple hammer, drove a spike into the head of General Sisera to literally pin him to the ground. Next, it would be the story of Queen Jezebel, thrown from her window and mauled by starving dogs, before their pups arrived and lapped up her black, still-warm blood. Plagued by fatigue and an acute sense of work well done – and disgusted by the sight of the dead skin building up under my nails in a dark collection of moist filth – three quarters of me would end up going to sleep. But my scrupulous index finger would mechanically do its work and my ears remained alert. Reformatory. Yael. Hammer. Dog. Jezebel. Reformatory. Rectify the situation. Critical situation.

As I scraped, the task would work its way into my dulled brain. I would already be dreaming. I was often a mole, sometimes a pneumatic drill or even a whole drilling rig. I would work away like this, until a heavy heel blow in the mouth encouraged me to finish my dream in my own room. My father long since gone to bed, I'd pull the cover a little way over the bad foot and leave Mother's room stealthily, blowing her a kiss, before sliding into my worm-eaten bed like a little snake, truly proud of my utility. One more night far from Apeca. I dreamt of a miracle. A miracle that would keep me away from it forever.

———

One afternoon, on my return from school, I saw my father at the kitchen door. He told me that he was going out on an errand, unhurriedly collected his wallet and the picture of his favourite horse, and walked out without looking back. He never returned. Except for his passport, nothing was gone from his drawers. His clothes, pale and discoloured, seemed to have retained only vague and contrasting memories of their owner – just like I had. When Mother understood, on the following day at around midnight, that he would probably not be coming home for dinner, she turned the house upside down. I thought she suspected him of being there, hidden somewhere between the fridge and the stove. Hysterical, and emboldened by her anguish, she shunted all the large furniture from one place to another. I felt I had to show some solidarity and started inspecting small appliances and the tableware. I lifted the teapot, turned back the bed sheets and rugs. I even checked the keyholes, plugholes and flower pots, always coming to the same worrying conclusion. Father was not in the toolbox, nor was he in the laundry basket! Nothing to report near the coffee maker; the cuckoo from the old clock certainly hadn't seen anything, and the cat swore that the only thing it had devoured was a sausage. The kettle water that I slowly poured down the sink washed away my last hope. If it had indeed been hiding in there, Father's slim and silent corpse would now be navigating the waters of the city's sewage system among the rats and fleas and the leftover pilchards.

Throwing a teary glance towards the mysterious vortex, I discreetly waved him goodbye: 'Bon voyage, pa! You'll never guess what they gave us for dessert today at school!' Alas, a great 'blurrrp' from the drain – both solemn and nonchalant at the same time – triggered a terrible fit of giggles in me; it seemed to confirm that Father was already sailing full speed towards all those other Baked Alaskas.

At dawn on the third day, the police station, the *gendarmerie*, the town hall, the morgue, the hospital and all the other institutions that Mother said had to be informed – that is to say everyone from the *préfecture* to the animal welfare charity, as well as the maternity hospital, the nursing home, the *conseil général*, the *conseil régional*, the chamber of commerce, the social welfare office and the neighbourhood's video library – were all let in on the secret. Afterwards she threw me in the back seat of the car, and we started searching the empty streets, the seafront, the farthest reaches of the indifferent city, for a dark man of medium height with short hair and no distinctive features.

This desertion soon became very public knowledge. In the city's packed squares, dark alleys and countless greasy spoons, people talked of nothing else. New bets were placed. Will he return? Won't he? Tonight? In a year? Never? Barmen would act as witnesses as fifty- or hundred-franc banknotes changed hands. Then, tantalized by doubt and curiosity, everyone swore they'd go and see the facts for themselves in the morning. Friends, neighbours and family wandered around our sitting room for a few days. They arrived, masked in solemnity and compassion, and conducted a thorough search of the papers on dad's desk. They took advantage of this opportunity to comment on our income, criticize our expenses and express surprise at our debts. They even got their hands on some medical reports. Around midday, their curiosity satisfied, they patted me on the head and warned me that if I didn't behave, Father would probably never come back or, if he did, it would only be so he could drop me off at You Know Where. Using this threat, they obtained a promise from me: I would be silent and subservient for the next fifty years. They then left the scene like the good, fat vultures they were, priding themselves on having provided moral support to a ruined family.

At the end of the seventh day, everybody stopped coming. We opened the windows wide to get rid of the sweaty smell of personal satisfaction and ill-hidden excitement that our friends had left behind.

Our family history ended then and there. And the entire universe started shaking beneath our feet.

For the first time, Mother recited a rosary of insults, pulled fistfuls of hair from her head and burst into tears. Out of consideration for her, I did the same. Staunch Christianity, Saturday trances, psalms offered up to Jesus Christ and even the threat of the reform school all became ancient history. Mother used her broom – the *balié nique* as we say in La Réunion – to chase away the two priests who had come to tell her that this was a mere trifle, that she would face many more trials – much more difficult, much more terrifying – like the death of her only child come Judgment Day if she did not let me go back to church next Saturday. Yahweh, farewell for all eternity!

Behind the thick wall that kept us well away from happiness, we were now two abandoned souls, two naked beings. The only noise was the gurgling of our famished entrails, accompanied, from time to time, by a torrent of uncontrollable sobs. Sometimes, everything was fine; otherwise we shed heavy tears and cursed my asthmatic and renegade father. From then on, a sort of silence reigned over us, the silence of a corpse in a tombstone, of a soul that loses its way and ends up in a breathless whirlwind of agitation. *A nervous breakdown*, as the English say. But there were still no English people to be found in this part of Saint-Benoît. Only their goddam pilchards! So we decided to use our own words – *Languèt ton momon!*[21] – which all

---

21  Reunionese insult. Possible translations: Deuce! Good heavens! By Jove! Oh anger, oh despair!

at once expressed our Dantean anger, our extreme disappointment, a wish never to have been born, and the unallayed fear of a future spent eating those horrible British sardines.

There was nothing more to be done – except to give oneself a hard pinch in order to wake from the nightmare. Yet alas, it wasn't a nightmare. But in a way, I had my revenge. I, too, began to say what I was thinking. I started attacking Mother and having a go at my runaway father who, I was willing to bet, would never come back. From morning to evening I could be heard. Out of the hundreds of bums on this island, Madame had to choose this one: a guy with no brains whatsoever, failure-bound before he was even born, though his natural inertia did amount to some kind of genius; a guy who grappled as much with his mucus as he did with his demons; a guy who mistook morning for night and slept until lunch! A guy who woke up at midday with a resounding 'Aahhhhhhh!', at once giving voice to his satisfaction with the previous night and his anticipation of the next one. I had only once seen such an advanced state of laziness before, in a species of giant panda from Cambodia. Long live the TV! At least it had shown me my father's ancestors.

Mother, as contrite as a cat caught with its paws in the fish tank, poured out insults and regrets in equal measure. She lamented having been starved from the age of twenty: mind you, she hadn't hungered for pilchards, but for happiness, for love and for freedom.

———————

In these cases people usually consult a psychoanalyst. At least that's what they do in Saint-Denis or Saint-Gilles-les-Bains. But for those of us in the east of the island, who are a more subtle, more intelligent breed with better imaginations, we have to pick out the right number – from all those our shameless friends have graciously left us. I'm not referring to the number of that useless Mental Health Centre, where the *Zoreils* haunt the corridors from dusk to dawn wanting to discuss their two-day-old dreams. I am not talking about lottery numbers either! No! When you are as pragmatic as a native of rue Descartes, the right number refers to the right *dévinèr*, a practitioner whose name you dare not utter! He – *li* – is Malabar at worst, Malagasy at best, but ideally Comorian. He is capable of bringing the dead back from beyond the grave and of freeing husbands from the clutches of any homewrecker. Any good – that is to say any bad – Reunionese worth their salt knew one. But to admit it and provide their address meant you held someone in the highest esteem. People would talk about *li* in a hushed voice so that others wouldn't find out. *Li* had to be kept secret, almost as if they could hear and cast a spell from afar. But, as a last-ditch attempt, when faced with your youngest's knotted hair or recurring gastroenteritis, a husband on the dole and a car that constantly broke down, you had to face the facts: neither the emergency department in Bellepierre Hospital nor the unemployment agency nor even the garage on the corner could offer a long-term solution. A duppy had been set on us. It was impossible to get rid of the bad luck we were stuck with without turning to *in bon dévinèr*.

'There be one in Les Hauts Mont-Vert. Him do a helluva job.'

'Me also hear there be one in Les Hauts Bras-des-Chevrettes. People say he amazing. With him, even the *Bébêt Djab* start running for him life!'

So you scrape together all your savings, you even do a little bit of Lenten fasting, and you eventually go there one morning before five, convinced that you will bump into no one and determined to get rid of this curse – or *fé noir* – cast upon you by an envious sister-in-law, a jealous brother, a rejected lover or an under-appreciated colleague. But you invariably arrive in a courtyard already packed with people and smelling of incense and goat. Chapel music or African drums play in the background. Eight or nine chairs are already taken – an epileptic here, a woman suffering from gout there. Next to her is another woman, six months pregnant, whose husband has left her for the school girl living one floor below them. A little further on, a group of men whisper. One of them wishes to bring harm to his boss simply because 'enough is enough'. Another is opening a snack bar and wants to make sure that the demon Asmodeus will act favourably towards it. The last man hopes he will get off scot-free from a sentence he is facing for driving under the influence. And what had he even done?! He'd only smoked two measly joints and then driven into three or four teenagers who had had the bright idea of ordering a *bouchon gratiné* [22] at a café terrace, when a sign clearly said that there were only tuna and sweetcorn sandwiches left. Had those cretins read the sign, he wouldn't be here at daybreak trying to negotiate the price of an early release and a black hen!

That's life on La Réunion: it passes from sorrow to spells, from petty vengeance to great supplication, from offerings to prayers. Poultry, *citrons galets,* [23] colour portraits and handfuls of coarse salt secure your future much more effectively than any savings account.

---

22  A sandwich *au gratin*, filled with steamed meatballs, chilli, mayonnaise, ketchup and grated cheese. The preferred dish of many teenagers in La Réunion.

23  Little citrus fruit ideal for casting an evil spell and curing a mid-season cold.

In any case, once the *dévinèr* has been paid, there isn't much left to save – but better to try than die in doubt.

If half of the Reunionese population sleeps at night, the other half – like those little grey crabs that rush to the beach of l'Hermitage by day – is busy playing the evil alchemist, calling out to all the divinities from the Hindu pantheon, imploring Lilith and Lucifer, invoking heaven and earth, crabs and periwinkles, Archangel Michael and Ganesh to try and ensure that all this evil (which has been wrapped up tightly in a thin plastic bag) disappears in the early morning, crushed under the tyres of the first car that fails to avoid it at a street corner.

'Anybody but me, Lord Vishnu! And please help heal me quick-quick!'

From now on, for the careless victim, it will be a question of thunderstorms, darkness and the abyss. His life will be a garland of unfortunate coincidences, a succession of obscene and disgusting encounters that no passers-by in the street will forget to comment on, whether it's to complain about it or approve of it. Best-case scenario, he will be able to hang himself; worst-case scenario, he will have to see another *dévinèr* who, to get rid of the spell he is under, will also fill a small non-recyclable plastic bag with turmeric, coconut and black hen's feathers and drop it at a street corner around midnight or quarter past. And this will go on and on. Another car will drive past, another victim will pay the price. The quacks get richer, the poor get poorer. Who cares if the street corners look like open-air kitchen cabinets, as long as the native is cured of all his ills.

So, on the day following a new moon, Mother and I gave it a go too. We went to a Comorian well versed in the business, and placed all our savings alongside the only photograph we had of dad on an old patchwork rug. Like all the other Comorians back then, his name was Saïd. Saïd was tall, thin and ugly; his eyes were black when the weather was nice and brown the rest of the year. His face was harsh, the lips pressed tightly together and the teeth yellowed from chewing tobacco. From under a furrowed brow, he stared with large, fierce eyes. He only walked on the tips of his toes, like a wild cat that has just stolen a big hunk of meat from the back of a butcher's. Did he have verrucas? Nobody knows, but his bouncy burglar's gait, which should have inspired absolute mirth, created incredible deference among his customers. People concluded that he was the best *dévinèr* there was. When Master Saïd made his entry, all wallets opened wide for him.

Sorcerer or not, he had a real talent: he could make anything he wanted disappear. Gone were our savings, our full-length portrait and even dad himself, whom Saïd was supposed to bring back to us. And prodigious professional that he was, he ultimately managed to push his genius to unprecedented heights: he made himself disappear too! Strangely though, all our other worries clung to us.

No longer able to pay rent, not knowing where we could seek refuge, we left our house and started leading a life of vagrancy between the mountain and the sea, living off the hospitality of a neighbour and the charity of the State.

It had taken Grandfather twenty-two years to get rid of a troublesome daughter, and he refused to take her back. And with a young daughter at that! Like the great philanthropist that he was, he lit a cigarette, spat out some mucus and cleared his throat, before heaping praise on the patience of his exemplary son-in-law. After calling us bitches, he eventually sent us seventy francs and a note full of spelling mistakes: 'I neva went to sea you a gain!' Mother cried twice as much as before, but my tears dried up when I realized that there were some banana-flavoured sweets in the envelope too. Grandfather wasn't that bad after all!

In the following weeks, we sold the small tortoises, half of our clothes and all of dad's. With the money we made, we settled at a one-eyed spinster's. She rented us a little house battered by the wind and eroded by the fetid sea-spray belched out by the ocean. The place was more of a shack than a mansion, but we were penniless. Our only other option was under the bridge over the Rivière des Marsouins (which was often in flood at this time of year anyway). That said, many would have preferred the river to this strangely furnished, comfortless place – and rightly so. Infested with mosquitoes, cockroaches and ugly objects, the house consisted of two small rooms. There was no running water or electricity, and there was only one window. It was as dark as it was filthy, although the former at least concealed the latter. It was lit by a candle that threw monstrous, shapeless forms on the cracked and mouldy walls – shadows that our minds, saturated by all kinds of superstitions, stirred into the most savage supernatural beasts such as the Tarasque.

All day long, like a good girl, I waited by the worm-eaten house for Mother's return. She would be carrying a bunch of leafy greens, insect larvae or cassava, anything to sate our hunger, which was as relentless as our despair. In the interval, our Cyclops-like host would take over and, under the pretence of getting to know me, would tirelessly question me about my deserter of a father, my now-irregular school attendance, Mother's misfortunes and uncaring grandparents. All of my answers would be rewarded with some hard, tasteless, out-of-date chocolate – a treat from last Christmas in July!

Most of the time though, Mother came back without work or provisions. Maybe she had spent the whole day crying under the pines at the seafront, turning over every pebble, wishing for a miracle. In vain. As on other evenings, she came back empty-handed, and we contented ourselves with three spoonfuls each of undercooked, white rice that reeked of cockroaches and bedbugs. We sat on the edge of the mattress in the light of an altar candle stolen from church and chewed on our scraps, with no pleasure, with no energy. One had to survive, though nobody had explained why.

I came to regret all the negative things I had said about those pilchards in tomato sauce. May God bless the English and their herrings!

How different children become once they experience poverty, bruises and a transformed appreciation of sardines. It's strange how quickly children can learn.

It was in this way that, at the age of nine, I grew old.

———————

After an interminable period – a hideous century, a hungry eternity to me – new hope seeded in the fertile soil of our suffering. A social worker found a crumpled folder at the bottom of a metal filing cabinet. It had been preventing the drawer from closing properly for two years already. Out of sheer curiosity, she took a look at the notes on the file. They provided our names and our miserable story. 'Oh great, another thing to take care of!' the young woman thought as she headed out for lunch.

Because the drawer worked properly now and because father had left us, we were owed some compensation. So the following week we said our goodbyes to the old Cyclops from the seafront and settled in a semi-detached house in the neighbourhood of Bras-Fusil. The State, like the good paternalistic provider it was, happily paid our rent and even our neighbour's – a single woman with five children to support. We added some furniture, did some painting, cultivated a lawn and planted a few flowers and some palm-tree seeds. And so began what in our later years we would refer to as the good old days. Before the Greens started to bother and browbeat us with their 'discard this here, recycle that there'. Those were the good old days indeed. For Mother and the other grown-ups, they were the days of government-subsidized contracts, the first deepfreezes, coach tours of the island on a Sunday, and hips swaying in nightclubs at La Plaine des Cafres. As for me, I was allowed to open wide the window of our brand-new car so I could throw out my empty lemonade bottle. I recall the hilarity of stuffing a lit firecracker into a chameleon's mouth, throwing our cat from the roof to confirm that they always land on their feet, grazing the doors of reversing cars while riding our bicycles without a helmet. Always happy even in sad times, between heaven and earth I wandered, a slingshot in my hand, completely intoxicated by the comfortable sweetness of life, by the endless repetition of this marvellous routine. For the young men too, those were the days: their first cigarettes, their first crushes, their first wrecked cars, which they'd try to fix for one, two, three months before concluding that wrecks they were and wrecks they would remain.

What are the good old days if not those times when you're satisfied with the little things and never feel alone, never feel far away? Living on housing estates: it was a brilliant idea that the State had hit on.

On paper, it means the quiet of the countryside and groves of hydrangea, shades of colour and bright canopies, friendship and mutual assistance. There are, for sure, some birds singing, a few cattleya orchids and one or two fireflies too. But no one is taken in. Living on a housing estate in La Réunion is absolute pandemonium – a living Hell. Everything is intimidating: the flowers called 'devil's trumpets', Daire Devil Street, the disreputable neighbourhoods of Bras-Fusil and Chaudron, and neighbours like Nabuchodonosor and Tombman. On a housing estate, the ants are red, the wasps are huge and nervy, the yappy little dogs are never on a lead or muzzled, and your neighbour is always serving a suspended sentence. There are stings, growls, barks. Things are out of control. In a nutshell, life on a housing estate is a mixture of creaaaaak, whap, boom boom, pop, brrrr, awwwwww. That is to say: creaking doors, well-deserved slaps, work on Sundays, a faulty amp and shaking roofs. And above all – above all else – mothers shouting and screaming at their three-year-old who has just dropped a couple of crumbs from their biscuit on the rather worn sofa. Mothers who are forced to take their gangster offspring by the scruff of the neck, shake them vigorously and give them a memorable slapping to teach them manners. 'You won't be a lazybones, my child!'

In short, life on a housing estate is noisy, poor, endless, but never dull or quiet. And if you happen to be bored despite it all, you can always plant a banana tree, a palm tree or a tree fern and watch it grow. That will help to pass the time.

———————

And time did pass quickly. One morning I realized that the palm tree in our garden was now well over ten centimetres above my head. Father was no more than a vague memory. Rumour had it that he was in El Salvador, Alaska, Timbuktu. At any rate, he was no longer in either our heads or our hearts. And Mother was working for the first time. Every day after school, you could see her on a zebra crossing, right in front of a red traffic light, a stop sign in her hand. With three other former representatives of the long-term unemployed, she formed an improbable barrier of good-natured souls that a hundred or so little tykes walked past in the morning, at lunch and in the afternoon as they made their way to class or back home. At first glance, it would seem she now had everything she needed to be perfectly happy. At first glance. Because if children are satisfied with very little, adults, on the other hand, are always looking for someone or something else. Mother's loneliness had sown the seeds of longing in her heart. Longing for a true, generous and eternal love – that's to say, an umpteenth adult idiocy! For we children know very well that the only true and eternal thing is Mistress Bélina – in other words, Father Christmas and his sack full of presents!

So, as they said back in those days, Mother tried to 'meet someone'. For months, I watched her comb through the classified ads in the Friday paper. Those dating ads in which half the Reunionese population reveal such wild desires that it takes the whole weekend for your mind to recover.

These small white rectangles in the daily paper are full of desire: people looking for great romances, a single-colour Rubik's cube, experiences with multiple partners and with no touching, a vinyl copy of the Pippin Apple and Lady Apple song. Their singular peculiarity makes you fear the worst about the mental health of their authors.

'*Que sera sera!*' Mother might have said, if she'd been able. But her limited vocabulary meant she had to settle for the equally eloquent 'Get it while it's hot!' – which left me very sceptical as I watched her, pink highlighter in hand, meticulously circling the most romantic advertisements. It was around that time she began to discreetly leave the house late every afternoon. Her small heels clicked on the tiled floor, her hair-straightener still plugged in on her dressing table. Everywhere her dress went, a tenacious smell of orange, vanilla and ylang-ylang lingered. She was behaving differently: her attention was elsewhere. She was distracted. 'I'll be back soon! Eat without me!' A hasty goodbye, and Madame was gone. Having been badly brought up, I spied on her through the window, like all the neighbours. During one of her afternoon escapades, I saw a car waiting for her at the entrance to the estate. So Mother had a chauffeur! But what was the point, since they stayed in that stupid parking spot, laughing about God knows what? Despite the tinted windows, I could see that the back seat was empty. There was plenty of space back there, so why the hell was Mother sitting on the chauffeur's lap?

One winter evening, the chauffeur got out of the car and barged into our house. From afar, he had seemed tall, professional and warm. Up close his boorishness became apparent; he gave off a strong smell of sweat and seediness. He sent a smirk in my direction and then didn't give me a second glance all evening. It was trendy back then to date mature women, prematurely single ladies who had one or two kids and a house where you could come and relax as much as you wanted to. He came every Saturday, emptied our cupboards and our wallet, and then sprawled in Mother's bed, demanding cigarettes. I made a habit of strolling by him, pinching and scratching him as hard as I could every time. Eventually, he officially declared that he'd had enough of this eleven-year-old attack dog lying in wait for him every weekend. After treating us to the world's choicest insults, he headed off and didn't look back. Truth be told, he'd found a better match – or *pied de riz* as we say here – in the neighbourhood next to ours. An old acquaintance of Mother's, as it turned out.

The door had barely closed behind him before another man – a musician this time, with a phony bohemian air – had settled in with his guitar and was asking for directions to the fridge. I showed him my best school reports, introduced him to Camille and Bélou, even cleaned his shoes. I would wake before dawn, often springing up to make sure that he was sleeping peacefully and had everything he needed, only to find my progress reports and dolls lying on the cracked tiled floor. I would pick them up sadly. Again, my new uncle left without a goodbye, without even taking the little guitar I had made for him using modelling clay and dental floss. Bring on the next in line!

A skinny, stooped suitor, with gaps between his teeth and root-deep decay. Rich, manipulative and calm, he was vicious to the core. He took pleasure in our misery and every Sunday morning would throw us a few crumbs from his vast fortune. But for this to happen, Mother had to abandon me every Saturday evening, following him into the dreadful depths of the night. I would yell, hide the car keys, beg them to stay or to take me with them. But to no avail. Mother would often fly into a rage and beat me half to death, taking advantage of my reduced state to tear the keys from my hands and leave. My heart torn to pieces, terrified of the voracious demons who ate sleepless children and temporary orphans, I slept with my arms tightly hugging my pillow, underneath which I had placed an old photograph of my mother, praying she would soon return.

A year, maybe two, went by. Again! And finally a fourth man entered the picture. Full of energy though very thin, cunning but not too bright, a compulsive liar and the most generous man you'd ever meet. He wasn't really any better than the bunch of crooks that had preceded him, but tired of fighting, I raised a white flag. After all, what higher hopes could I have entertained for my almost illiterate mother? She'd gone soft in the head, and had big flabby breasts and a young child. No doctor, no senior official, no man with any level of education, however minimal, would have wanted her.

The new incumbent did receive a few slaps and a couple of kicks and pinches as welcoming gifts, but after a couple of years, I began to tolerate his presence. I had the feeling that he hated me less than the others did. Here were some squinting eyes in which I would exist. At last!

Grateful, I decided to endure him, and everything about him, including his 'little problem'. Now, what the Dessaintes called a 'little problem' would be for others a cause for immediate divorce or redundancy without notice, if not a fixed prison sentence. But in our family, our expectations were set so low that anyone was welcome in our world. Who were we to judge? And that is how Lucien and his 'little problem' entered our lives.

The 'little problem' he struggled with was rampant alcoholism punctuated by weekly ethylic comas, incredible mythomania and halitosis that would awaken old Bukowski himself. But because, in a pause between two bottles of rum, this fourth fellow asked about my scholarly achievements, I decided to turn a blind eye to his 'little problem' and the rest of his scrappy, dysfunctional life and ended up concluding that these flaws were insignificant. That his affection mattered more than anything else. One day, before getting plastered, he gave me six volumes of an old, worm-eaten encyclopaedia, swearing with his hand on his liver that he'd just bought them. From then on, only shyness and the fact that I was out of the habit prevented me from calling him 'papa'. Despite his mediocrity, I believe I loved this fourth suitor and that he had no qualms about becoming my father. There were several traces of a profound humanity left in him: he was generous, enthusiastic and unintentionally funny. So what did it matter that two sets of hands were needed to carry him to Mother's bedroom – one to hold his feet, the other to hold his arms! What did it matter that he had absolutely no idea how he'd ended up at our house the next day! I had a father. That was what mattered the most.

Every other day, Lucien would come into our teak-furnished sitting room, beset by delirium tremens. With the wholehearted gusto of a provincial schoolmaster, he'd stammer out promises about how we'd live like royalty. No one else had ever made us a better offer, so his bluster gained our vote. It wasn't much. And yet it was. The world is such a mess.

Lucien was as uncultured as he was boastful, the latter quality at least masking the former by providing him with a professorial air. In the beginning, unaccustomed as I was to being around men of learning, I saw him as an incomparably intellectual figure. And the guarantee of excellent school results. But my awe faded when he started helping me with my homework. I kept failing my assignments, and very quickly my fascination with him turned into amazement at myself. How could I have believed in him in the first place? This was followed by a sense of defiance and, ultimately, utter indifference to all his verbiage. But the interest he showed in me was genuine. In our miserable lives, he became everything to us and we became everything to him. For once, a human being was invested in my scholarly success; it was completely out of the question for this state of affairs to come to an end! That's where I got the idea of working really hard, of persevering, and of succeeding in school. It was a way to show him my gratitude, and a way to continue to attract his praise.

At the end of each term, with my report card between my teeth, I would fly to his place, narrowly escaping being run over by a car at least ten times. I was filled with and lifted by – but most often tormented by – the need to exist in someone's eyes. Anyone's. Including this shameless drunk's. I would arrive covered in sweat and would brave the ferocious dog that guarded his villa, knocking over three or four garden gnomes in my frenzied race to survive, to gain fame and recognition. I'd enter without knocking and – despite my torn clothes, my tear-filled eyes and my shaking body – feign the most complete sangfroid, adopting a detached tone and a studied nonchalance, which were the exact opposite of my interior ebullience. The sacred report would be covered with sweat, rabid dog drool and bits of terracotta gnome, and I'd disdainfully throw it on the table, saying: 'Oh, by the way, now that I come to think of it, here's my report card, if you want to have a quick look.' And then I'd promptly pass out. But Lucien was wise enough never to make fun of me. When I came around, I'd be welcomed with a glass of gone-off orange juice and some stale biscuits. I would wolf them down and then resume my race to conquer the world, spurred on by the sensation I had then – that I could reach out and touch the sky. Without him ever knowing, I made a solemn promise to us both: I would pass the end-of-year exam with flying colours. All the love I'd had for my cold-hearted mother was now shifted to a more loving recipient. I studied early in the morning, at the dead of night, for entire afternoons – in the local public library, at the school library, under the city bus shelters. In short, everywhere and at all times, as long as Mother didn't notice. Three months before the moment of truth, I was already good to go. I couldn't wait to place the precious certificate on my admirer's table. He himself had never obtained it, and I became the instrument of his revenge. Restless and hungry for success, we were like two starving wolves patiently stalking our prey.

It was around that time that Lucien was found dead at the foot of the stone stairs to his villa. 'Dead drunk'. The expression couldn't be a better fit. When we arrived, the life had already started to leave his body in great drops. It flowed out of his inebriated heart and into the damp earth. The sky was reflected in his dull and distant eyes, which looked both surprised and angry. The Grim Reaper had come too soon. For the first time in my life, I shed bitter tears at someone's death.

———————

Even my grandparents' death hadn't affected me to such an extent. Quite the opposite! I was so indifferent to the news that on the very evenings of their funerals I could be heard singing a song. Grandmother had died as she had lived: with the complete disinterest of mankind. Even though she'd brought twelve children into the world, her first sixty years were unnecessarily long, arid and dull; spent amid the heat of a smoking stove, blows to her ribs and daily rape. Once the children had gone, and menopause and arthritis had set in, Grandfather left the house too. He felt no remorse about having worn her to the bone and was convinced she wouldn't live much longer. Her breasts heavy, her cheerfulness gone, her dignity stripped from her by decades of miscarriages and servitude, Grandmother locked herself up in her tin house in Sainte-Marie. From then on, she devoted herself, body and soul, to a flower garden where her nasturtiums, flamingo flowers, red flag bushes and parrot flowers grew in lush abundance. While waiting for her green shoots to show, she discovered a benevolent God to whom she confessed all her sorrows. One morning, among her peace lilies and wild sage, she had an epiphany and cried out: 'Lord Jehovah!' The unnatural joys, the debased humanity, the stench of Grandfather's adultery, the unspeakable misery that her children had gone through … her existence was worth about as much as a child's drawing. So to spare herself the yoke of eternal bitterness and regret, she decided to forget everything. Including her own name and those of her grandchildren. Her new craze was to walk along the dual carriageway by Gillot Airport at sunset, from Sainte-Marie towards La Possession, asking the drivers who stopped if they could take her to Mauritius where she had arranged to meet some Jim bloke. An ambulance or the fire brigade would take her back home. As soon as she arrived in front of the locked gate of her house, she'd burst into tears for no reason. The paramedics on call prescribed her rest and a daily dose of chamomile tea, since her garden was full of it. Less than a year later, on the only day that her carer arrived an hour late, she died. There was a smile on her lips and a bouquet of daffodils in her hand.

Grandfather, delighted to have outlived her, swore that he had never loved her. Every afternoon, he went from one tea dance and one decrepit dowager to another. Two months after Grandmother's funeral, he married a spinster, Mademoiselle Agnès, who had very few teeth and a dubious sense of humour, but who was as rich as Croesus and as salacious as could be. They got drunk on cognac together and sang bawdy songs for hours on end. Their children, alerted by exasperated neighbours, would hurry over to confiscate their liquor and music. It was high time to stop this nonsense and study the *Ars moriendi* in silence! The calm would last for a couple of days; they could even be seen quietly placing a large candle and two peonies before the Black Virgin of the Rivière-des-Pluies.[24] But on the third day, they'd plunge into an abyss more muddy and wanton than ever, dip into a textbook on black magic called the *Petit Albert*, and participate in big orgies in the jungle around Grand Étang. This went on for fifteen years. Then, tired of these licentious activities, but still hungry for new acquaintances, they turned to religion, started worshipping Saint Peter, read the gospels every day and eventually found an old Jesuit to offer them absolution. Grandfather continued to relieve himself of his sins once a year and died one ordinary morning, muttering in the dim light of the confessional. His death felt like good news. His drawers were emptied, his clothes collected and, together with his syphilitic

---

24   The Black Virgin is a very famous place of worship located in the neighbourhood of Rivière-des-Pluies, in the North East of La Réunion. Believers love the place as it is the location of the only Black virgin on the island. She is associated with a legend of slavery.

and diabetes-ravaged body, everything that had belonged to him was cremated without a word. When it was all over, a hurried hand threw his ashes into a secluded corner of the cemetery in Sainte-Marie.

Mother, who'd been at war with both my grandparents, had never deemed it necessary to introduce me. So the only images I had of them were of grotesque mummies, stiff and cold and lying in the middle of an unfurnished room. The day I met them, they were already dead. And yet Mother made sure to turn this occasion into a frightful experience. Why change a losing team? So, at the age of eleven, I was pushed towards my grandmother's statue-like body. Go and give her a kiss! I walked half-heartedly, my knees shaking, towards this ghostly face shrouded in white lace. As I drew nearer, I was terrified that when I bent down to give her a kiss, Grandmother would suddenly sit up and bite me. When my lips finally reached the lace, I felt something icy-cold move slowly. I don't know what happened next. I blacked out. When I regained consciousness, Mother told me that Grandmother, whom I had imagined was floating across the Styx, had not actually been dead. She'd only been asleep, but when she saw that I had passed out like the rotten progeny I was, the disappointment had killed her.

---

Our war carried on and we were well matched, Mother and I. We had one thing in common at least: each of us employed equal determination, equal energy. I wanted an education, she wanted to discourage me from everything. If I got brilliant results and received my teachers' congratulations? I was the paragon of a Reunionese *harki*, in support of complete assimilation, wanting – let's face it! – to be even more European than the British themselves. If my results were average or poor? It was thanks to my laziness, my tendency to exaggerate intellectual capacities which, clearly, I didn't have and would never acquire. School was not meant for people like us! No matter how hard I worked, I was always destined to fail. The Dessaintes had never succeeded in anything anyway. They die ignorant: that's their fate! I started out with nothing, except for my obsessive wish to rehabilitate Cain's race and the vice known as reading.

I read everything. Maupassant, Cicero, Hesse and Rostand. Süskind and Mirbeau. Loti, Melville, Seneca, Lautréamont, *À rebours*, Lao She and Livy. Anything that could be used as a door wedge or paper weight. Anything that would otherwise be easy fuel when we ran low on candles on the night of a cyclone. Lots of comics too. I would have sold my father for a *Picsou Magazine* or a *Mickey Parade Géant*. This universe of coloured speech-bubbles where the evil characters are not really that bad has never left me: the characters are just brainless individuals with clenched fists – a little narcissistic, a little complicated – who want to conquer the world out of sheer stupidity and boredom. So when nothing's going right, when the walls get so high that even prayers can't help you scale them, I open a comic book. As if leaning over a precipice, I dive right in, seeking a different world where no one can find me and I can forget. I have a book on my bedside table. Because I don't have a gun.

---

Perhaps friendship would have taken away my precocious nihilism. But I have made hardly any friends since the start of secondary school. Not for a lack of trying: a few very awkward words exchanged. One day, a girl declares 'You are like us', but from that moment I no longer am. Anyone who saw my breasts – like the udders of a Friesian heifer – and my bulldozer lips would excuse Saint-Benoît's crème de la crème and their daily oscillation between frank camaraderie and the coolest contempt for me. Sometimes they call me the camel; sometimes they call me nothing at all. They like me for two days. On the third, they point their fingers at me. But eventually they always send me packing – just not right away. First they tell me exactly what they think of me. Never out of nastiness. It's always for my own good. I ought to know. Nothing escapes them, not even my clothes. They are as rough and ugly as an old maid's. I'm badly brought up. I'm not funny. I talk too much; I don't communicate enough. I lack confidence; I'm too sure of myself. I have a guilty conscience; I'm forever playing the victim. I see the dark side of everything; I'm too optimistic. I misunderstand everything; I understand nothing. I'm the worst. I'm unbelievable. I feel ashamed, and my heart grows as heavy as a boulder: I'm nobody's equal. I apologize profusely. But it's too late. They no longer forgive my existence. I'm a dog; I want to beg. For a single glance. To be included. Please give me a friend. Let me lie at their feet. I'm scared they'll desert me. That would kill me. But I remain alone, everywhere. I have no friends other than Camille and Bélou. I'm surrounded by girls who are in love, girls who are wanted. Hot-headed, meticulously styled, ultra-perfect adolescents are all around me. They like each other one week, they kiss the second, the passion dies in the twilight of the third, but unlike me, they are never alone. They're happy and carefree, blessed at all times, and that's what adolescence is all about. How can I bear a grudge against them? For what? For being too well born to have empathy, to be friendly? I remain just outside their range of vision at school – there's no hatred. Their daily denigrations convince me to accept my total insignificance. I'm doomed to follow at a distance; I'll never even play a supporting role.

These repeated rejections engendered an increasingly bitter air of abandonment in me. The sense of failure I felt became so agonizing that it destroyed my will to live. Deprived of the smallest scraps of friendship, every encounter bruised me a little more. I would go home bewildered, alone, harbouring a terrible feeling of defeat. I had just one idea: to kill myself rather than endure this quagmire. That's how the beast is born: alone, wounded, already in agony. Lugging along her pain and an eternal urge to do battle, she is animated by a single breath – despair.

———————

I did very little in the following three years. I was in mourning for Lucien during my remaining time at school. I reshaped the world to my liking – or rather, I created one to fit my dimensions. A world both full and desolate, populated by immortal writers already in their graves. A world circumscribed by cloud, with prospects so limited that they are reduced to a single notion: the ultimate liberty of a quick, heartfelt suicide. I don't know how I was able to live in such extreme sorrow, permanently waiting for somebody to appreciate me but meeting with continual disappointment. To be honest, it's terribly wearisome, constantly wearing a mask of gaiety to prevent anyone from noticing your grimace of nameless suffering

– you no longer have any idea what you are living for. You're forced to repress an insane desire to scream out that you're being murdered, that you're down on the floor, that it's too late, you're done for. It is death and defeat, not life, that seem to make sense from where you're standing in the world.

I'd like a death as violent as burning. To have the courage to tear out my veins with my teeth. I'd like to slice open my belly with a knife – that's how much I loathe this popular belief that life is for living. Were it not for writing, I'd have abused this body as if it was a slave, drowned it in a sea of barbiturates. I want to cause myself pain, because I'm already suffering and nobody has come to save me. I want to give up rather than tolerate the cruelty of the world and its daily trifles. But I'm cowardly. I take a step forward and I feel scared. I give up and change my mind. So I'm obliged to live. Though I'm scared stiff. And I despise myself for being a chicken. If I have to die, I will die! Provided it's violent. In other words, I'm full of faith but exhausted by trying; I'm determined to die precisely because life renounces the spineless and is sacred. I remain full of determination, energy and alacrity – I don't want to die young and unfulfilled. I'm looking for a goal, an understanding, to be useful for someone or something. To find the way, or rather to plot it out.

———————

At sixteen and a half, ahead of a multitude of careless chatterboxes, I came second in my class. You never know your luck. But I was forced to face a new adversary, who was just as cunning and just as tough as Madame Dessaintes. She was top of the class and, incidentally, the cause of all my troubles. She was a proud and arrogant young person. She always wore lipstick, and the teachers lived only to indulge her. She was constantly stretching out her neck haughtily to accept their praise. In a singular fit of compassion for the exotic, her family – direct descendants of the Grand Dukes of Aquitaine – had felt like discovering southern lands, their anaemic rabble and their virgin forests.

At Mass on Sunday, the bishop of Bordeaux had one day held forth at great length on Ethiopian eunuchs, equality between the races, tolerance and love for one's fellow man.

'Those Blacks!' he screamed into a feeble microphone, setting his silk skullcap trembling. 'Even if we don't know why God created them, those Blacks exist all the same. So they are your equals.'

Equality. Why not? The following week, eight of Bordeaux's inhabitants jumped into an aeroplane and eleven hours later landed in the middle of the island which, behind closed doors, they still called Bourbon. They had only planned to spend a month there, but in their absence – due to the death of the paternal grandfather – a sordid inheritance matter disturbed their habitual sangfroid. Suddenly – down the phone and by post – various illegitimate offspring and adulterers were revealed. Then came a time when all the gossip magazines devoted a weekly insert to the quarrels of the Tervilliers-Brichaudys: longstanding incestuous relationships; former collusions with the brownshirts; suspect increases in wealth; the bestial extravagances of the dead grandfather. It was all exposed in successive articles sold at a laughable price even in the newsagents of the Mascarene Archipelago. The family knew they were ruined – everything was true. So in one voice, without consulting each other, they said, 'It's all up. Come on, have some guts! Let's hide!' They then sequestered themselves – not for a few weeks, but for dozens of months – in the elegant western neighbourhood of the town of Saint-Benoît, where, from four o'clock every afternoon, life can be put on pause.

The mother, an old lady tormented by gout, read a great many books on the local flora and went out for walks. But after three weeks, weary of the rain, the gossips, the heat, the Blacks, the humidity of the air, the mosquitoes, the unemployed, the sun, the wind, the sea spray, the mountains, the dengue fever, the stray dogs and the traffic jams, she holed up in her sitting room, her feet plunged in a bowl of salty water, and explored the world through a television screen. Her contact with the natives was limited to the imperatives she communicated to the gardener and home help once a week. Convinced of the vulgarity and laziness of the island's hoi polloi, she socialized only with a small set of carefree, cigar-smoking bureaucrats and bons vivants who, on Saturday evenings fortified by sundowners, took themselves off to explore the young and amenable native women. Her devotion to these people was absolute.

Full of nostalgia for hunting with hounds, the father vented his melancholy on bevies of deer in the ravenala forest. When he wasn't occupied with this, he met up with a young woman with long, slender, bronzed legs, to whom, between kisses, he recounted the infinite emptiness of his marriage. He wanted to marry her, if only to no longer feel his wife's clammy legs crushed against his knees in bed every night. At the first signs of old age, gathering all his courage, he fled the elegant family villa and moved into the working-class neighbourhood of Bras-Fusil. Despite its off-putting name, he lived there happily with his new companion, her two little brothers, their parents, an old aunt who'd had her left leg amputated, two yappy little dogs and a chameleon.

After three months, having given communal living a good try, he delicately kissed his mother-in-law's hand, apologized twice, then gathered together his wife's belongings and those of the reptile, and went off to settle with them in a colonial manor more worthy of his rank, in the shade of the great flamboyant trees of Bourbier-les-Hauts. Despite his new life, twice a day he would drop off and then pick up his daughter from the secondary school in town. He had called her Constance-Zéphyrine! Imagine giving such a ridiculous name to a little stinging nettle!

It was in my final year that I came to know that nasty little piece of work. She arrived with a graceful, extremely self-assured step, took a seat in the first row and emptied her thermos flask of lotus tea in little sips. This flask never left her side. From time to time, she took a few notes or finished a novel, and she passed all the planned and unannounced tests that posse of lecturers imposed on us regularly, the devil knows how. To complete our humiliation, the teachers never failed to photocopy and distribute plentiful copies of her irreproachable work, peppered with 'Ah!', 'Oh!', 'Marvellous!', 'Remarkable!' and other dithyrambic obscenities in red, which showed the extent to which those wretches had swooned – hand on heart with a feverish brow – upon reading her literary hotchpotch. We others, the remaining thirty-five students, barely cast an eye on it. Ugh! It reeked of pomposity and bookish brown-nosing! If, even inadvertently, a curious individual slipped one of those blasted scripts into their exercise book, they were vilified at breaktime. They were clowns! Defectors! They'd the imaginations of trained monkeys.

----

In those days, geography essays were written on Wednesday mornings, in a study hall overlooking the ocean. Five minutes before the start of the test, a supervisor with slicked-back hair – his nickname was Silly Billy – made his entrance. He approached each student in his hideous way, hunched and with a heavy step. When he handed out the papers, his fingers left a dreadful greasy whitish film in the corner of each sheet. As he ambled along each row, the sour odour of his sweat hovered. It lingered at each table, travelling up the nostrils, before mixing with and then entirely obscuring the floral notes of the young girls' perfume. When we began to write, there remained only a vague smell of decayed flowers in the classroom. Billy then perched himself at the teacher's desk and, pretending to read the two-day-old newspaper, fell into a deep sleep. Four hours later the emphatic rustle of the Zephyr's script indicated that time was up. She was always the first to leave. Fresh as an orchid, she seemed to have worked with effortless inspiration, her gaze caressing the sea, a cup of steaming tea constantly within reach of her long, slender fingers. She was a serene and erudite nymph with flowing locks, and each of her nonchalant movements gave off an exquisite fragrance of geranium that could waken the entire town, except old Billy. Faced with these blatant provocations, it's hardly surprising that the other thirty-five dreamed only of murdering her. Her place was right in front of mine, which was perfect for plunging something into her back – a sabre, a compass, my set square, a chair, anything at all, provided it was fatal and that death was very long and painful. I could see her pen delicately dancing from one page to the next, following the rhythm of her muses. The result was predictable: nine pages full of nonsense, an umpteenth twenty out of twenty, a grotesque panegyric from the teacher and another humiliating defeat for everyone else.

Our people demanded revenge at any cost. What were we? Rogues? Indolent scoundrels, dunces in tracksuits? For how long would we have to suffer these insults? Aagh! What a curse to have such blind and incompetent teachers! What about their supposed impartiality? The dignity of a class and, by extension, an entire people was at stake. I gathered my courage, determined to avenge our honour and get one over on Tervilliers-Brichaudy. One Wednesday morning, I raised myself up a few centimetres, craned my neck and tried to copy as many sentences as I could from the script of that beanpole. These acrobatics went on for nearly three hours. Then, defeated by a stiff neck and the start of a muscle cramp, I was forced to postpone our vengeance until later. The result? Just one paragraph in four hours. True to habit, old Billy collected up all the scripts and, still groggy with sleep, shuffled off to slip them into the teacher's pigeonhole. That day though, one thing was different: I was right behind him! The school was one of the few in town not to have lessons on Wednesday afternoons, so the staff room was as empty as their heads. Once I was sure old Billy was gone, I made a beeline for the precious pigeonhole. I removed the bundle of scripts, pulled out mine and put the others back in their place. The hoops they made me jump through, these amateur babysitters!

Returning home, emboldened by this initial victory, I gathered up a pile of blank sheets of paper, several pens and half a dozen works on history and geography, and I sat down to continue my composition. For, come what may, I wanted to keep trying to do the right thing. 'Overseas territories in the context of globalization: an unequal form of integration': that shouldn't be too difficult seeing as a certain show-off had drawn an entire novel from it. The first three hours felt like one. Tense and determined, I highlighted several books at a time, consulted my exercise book, quoted Tervilliers-Brichaudy, prepared a rough sketch, drew up a glossary. They'd soon see! At the end of the fourth hour, I began to lose my head a little. In front of me, a new paragraph of indigestible ideas had barely progressed at all. It was closer to claptrap than to the composition of the century. At the close of the fifth hour, I opened a second ream of paper. On the ground, the sheets from the first – now shreds of paper, angrily scattered round the room – looked like large snowflakes blown off course. After six hours, tearing out my hair with one fist, I used the other to dry the fat tears that were wetting the sole page of writing I'd done. Six hours of uninterrupted work just for that. All that remained was for me to hope that Tervilliers-Brichaudy had, this time round, experienced as many difficulties as I had. And I secretly hoped that her work was at best vastly off topic and at worst one of those twenty-page digressions that would permanently raise suspicions about her true identity as an empty-headed cacographer.

Admittedly I had only written a single page, but with what panache! And with what ardour! Suffice to say that between the girl from Bordeaux's waffle and my one page, there wouldn't only be a difference of 19 points revealed but an entire universe!

However, the reality of my mediocre past grades drained my optimism. What if this pen-wielding Medusa emerged triumphant again? What a blow for the rest of us! Damn! Fortune followed her as a dog does its master. This time, I had to make sure to follow the dog. Her script! I needed her script! My face lit up with inspiration. Hah! Nobody would find out. Expeditus, patron saint of emergencies and lost causes, help me! I slipped into my shoes and, like a petty thief, rushed back to the school. At that hour – as at all others, incidentally – it was as wide and empty as the caldera on the Piton de la Fournaise on the day of an eruption. I entered the staffroom, looked in the accursed pigeonhole and retrieved the script belonging to Constance-Zéphyrine. I needed no more than half an hour to make the return trip, the essay in my hand.

Even if it was only a jumble of nonsense, it was nonetheless nonsense that was beautifully presented. No crossing out, not a single trace of rubber, no ink stains. The writing was neat, graceful, immediately comprehensible. I read her drivel in a single sitting. 'What the devil!' I exclaimed when I reached the end. The *Zoreil's* work was perfect! Perfect in every way! It was the height of erudition. Each page was studded with pedantic quotations, slick assertions and examples plagiarized from goodness knows where. There was no doubt about it! This immaculate dissertation writer had the memory of an elephant and a prodigious eloquence. As for me, my head was spinning. Terrible geniuses like this – incapable of pronouncing a single Creole word – should be sent into exile on Tromelin Island! Why not send them to the Scattered Islands, these schoolyard intellectuals who quote Malte-Brun at the drop of a hat but don't know a single *séga* singer? What are we waiting for? Nietzsche, Heidegger and Vidal de la Blache don't add up to anything greater than our *rougail saucisse* – our sausage stew.

The essay was so beautifully written that – like a true Giuseppe Baldini of the tropics – it seemed immoral *not* to borrow the principal passages. Oh, and then copying out half of it seemed right and proper … I wasn't ransacking it; I was legitimately collecting tithes. We had welcomed her in, we had put up with her: she owed it to us. Debt collecting done, I went to sleep around midnight, wholly satisfied by the efficient execution of my mission. The next day I was up before anyone else. I snuck into the staffroom and placed the two perfect essays in the pigeonhole as if nothing had ever happened.

Two weeks later, in the most degrading of ceremonies, Mistress Islander, our old history and geography teacher, handed out the scripts, as usual starting with the best. 'Ter …!' That was all. Scarcely had she uttered this first syllable than I was overcome by a strange and ambiguous sensation. I suddenly found myself completely ridiculous, mediocre – detestable. Though they were no more than a small group of letters of no great consequence, this murmur violently plunged me into an arid and unknown atmosphere in which a dense plume of sadness arose in small wafts. As time itself withered away around me, this devastating 'Ter …' ceaselessly echoed in my head. It lasted a thousand years, an eternity of single seconds, during which the entire universe was merely an enigmatic 'Ter …'. 'Ter …' marked both the beginning and the end. Then there was something that resembled silence; a pre-war truce. Before I had managed to regain my self-control, another thunderous volley was launched. Was I dreaming? Was I in the grip of a fever? This time, I heard 'Villiers …' as if from nowhere. I had instinctively retained some form of hope up to this point, but a sharp cold shudder now extinguished any last vestiges that remained. I rubbed my eyes, then my ears. I was plunged into the darkest disillusionment. I had lost so much faith in myself that I didn't even think about crying. Defeated! Yet again!

My grand designs lay in ruins. That day, my name was the last to be called out. Geography really was not my forte. Nor was the role of tax collector. Being a peaceable soul, despite my tenacity – what is euphemistically termed a brat – I decided to temporarily hide myself away between a houseplant and an empty cupboard.

Lucien dead; the Tervilliers-Brichaudy damsel alive and well. My experience put things beyond doubt: existence was merely a huge betrayal, with obstacles and disappointments of all kinds scattered through it. With something in me missing, I finished my exam preparations under a funerary sky, in the tepid solitude of May. And to think that all my personal trials would not even yield one extra point in the final exams!

The final exams – the *bac*! Let's talk about them! On the day itself, or rather three weeks beforehand, all the secondary school students are in a kind of trance. The alarmists shout, they scream, they fast, they abstain from everything – even sleeping. They try to learn off by heart, in one night, the contents of the key books they haven't read – in other words all of them. The defeatists – red in the face, impatient, feverish and hypersensitive – are already mentally composing the letters they'll send to contest their results. Every morning, the students come into class as if it's an agricultural fair. They're noisy, frantically chatty; you can make out one or two pleasantries and pathetic worries about the exams in the hubbub. Even during lessons, the room hums with new obsessions: success, first time, big binge!

At one twenty in the afternoon, laughter is spreading through the class. It pours out into the corridor and ripples along the ramp where the teacher is just arriving. Outside, a dong, dong, dong summons late arrivals, both schoolmasters and students, to their classrooms. A moment's silence. The teacher comes in. Smiles fade and are replaced by the most serious of airs. The atmosphere changes completely: the boys readjust their flannel shirts, the girls tame their hair, urgent hands close the windows. Everyone settles down and stares at this little old man in shirt sleeves. He greets the usual bootlickers in the first row with a smile and takes some inky sheets of paper out of his satchel. An infernal commotion begins. Er! Sir! Sir! We haven't finished the syllabus! Sir! Sir! When will we finish the syllabus? Sir! Sir! What's the point of the syllabus? On the load-bearing wall, in a wooden frame, Bucephalus, whom Alexander is trying in vain to calm, is whinnying violently, threatening to break out of his Macedonian stall and flee to our tropical version of Santorini. At the back of the class, the star of the show herself looks worried under her little silk cap. Will we finish? Won't we finish? Forty minutes of endless discussions, fifteen proper minutes of class. Luckily, I don't attend very often.

The morning of D-Day, I could be found kneeling beside a half-empty bucket in a pensive mood, sponging up the vomit from an umpteenth night of maternal drinking. Lucien had been dead for three years. Mother had now been an alcoholic for a very long time. Suffocating in the sour stench of drunkenness, I saw my decade and a half of aimless existence reflected in the bottom of the pail, but for once, I didn't vomit up my entire innards. It seemed to me that I had two hearts, two giants that carried me from one suffering to the next with rash, insatiable determination despite the slings and arrows of outrageous fortune. I left the house and my semi-comatose Mother at around eight, feverishly resolved to take no prisoners. On the other side of town, the philosophy exam was waiting for me.

Nobody on the estate had ever succeeded in triumphing over the *bac*. Some spoke of it deferentially, while others simply cursed the two weeks of fierce battle and their always disastrous after-effects. With the exception of Mother, without really believing it could happen, everyone was living in hope of a miracle – a miracle of daring and revenge that would wash away, even just once, the infamy of our centuries of defeat. This is the aspiration of those who have nothing left except plenty of misfortune and a few castles in the air. Good luck, eh! Don't give up! You'll get there in the end! Once again, the betting resumes and fifty-franc notes are passed back and forth just like at the market in Saint-Paul.

Though they don't know it, I fashioned all of this into a solid breastplate and marched on the school armed to the teeth. After all, how could anything worse happen to us? Each day, my anger served as a tonic, as an increasingly vicious retaliation, a shield against defeat. Like a spur in my flank, it made me stay right until the end of each exam. And my zeal enjoyed its reward. A victory snatched from the mean grip of destiny. The *bac* passed with distinction, the admiration of an entire neighbourhood, praise from my old teachers. It was just compensation for entire weeks sitting on a terrace exposed sometimes to wind, sometimes to music, sometimes to the infernal fanfare of the television, wearing out my brain as I crammed it full of civil wars, world wars, cold wars, nuclear wars, submarine warfare, manoeuvre warfare, attrition warfare, trench warfare. What a lot of grief for one certificate! What a terrible spate of solitude for a single day of recognition!

During my revision, anxiety attacks had drowned me in floods of tears. Like any school child, desperate for confidence, indulgence and consolation, I went to Mother in search of some courage. Please be a mother, just for once. For one day. I don't need love! A little pity. A miniscule amount. A teeny weeny bit. Is it too much to ask?

All I got was a torrent of shouts, reproaches and disappointment. Those teachers? Those books? I should just tell them all to bugger off – the brothel-reared sons of bitches. I should use their inky rags to wipe my arse! Why did I always aspire to things that were beyond me? What crap! When would I understand that all that wasn't for us? Books and pens should be left to their queer kids or to those *zouk* dancers from the Antilles!

In fact, the Antilleans did become better writers than us, but then they weren't smashed into smithereens as soon as they were old enough to hold a pen. But that's another story.

For the time being, each of us was silenced, both stunned and incensed by the strangeness of the other. Who are you, Mum? Where did you come from, my little girl? Despite our shared human form and the same mud flowing in our black blood, all conversation was impossible. Every time it ended in the same disappointment.

During the two or three weeks following my achievement, I was praised on several occasions, but as soon as Mother appeared, our friends and neighbours would muzzle their pride. We resumed our habitual boorishness as if nothing cataclysmic had happened. As if there had been no revolution. No, for Mother it was nothing! Or to be more precise, this nothingness was an abomination. In her mind, all parents traumatized by a past in which they were constantly made to stand in the corner of the classroom needed to be avenged. Children should share the same crude, clear-cut and incurable loathing for school. More than that! I should have taken retaliatory measures. I should have boycotted school, whipped the bare behinds of those teachers whose parents had humiliated her, before hanging them by the neck over a great bonfire of exercise books, pencil cases and school textbooks. Now, to tell the truth, we children did have these plans in mind – but only the day before written tests! If we scored well, the teachers and inspectors became our best friends. Having fraternized with the enemy, I could no longer count on her support. I had gone over to the other side. The bad side. So there were no congratulations or celebrations that July evening when I announced, shamefaced, that I had gained a distinction.

Not knowing how I might ever make up for this umpteenth offence, I appeared before Mother late and trembling, ready to invoke the administrative chaos characteristic of exam periods to excuse my crime. I'd hardly even written anything down, I'd say, so I couldn't possibly have got more than five or six out of twenty! The results couldn't be mine. I'd renounce them vehemently; I'd get indignant about the incompetence of these amateur exam boards. If those were my real grades, let them burn me alive! In a few days, it would all be forgotten and, knowing Mother, she would never demand any proof of my failure. But when the moment came, I didn't need any of the stories I'd prepared. Madame Dessaintes had pulled out all the stops once again.

When I got home, I found Mother half-naked, stuffed full of pills and alcohol, and unconscious. The doctor hesitated before he gave his verdict: 'Either a suicide attempt or an accidental overdose.' It was the second time. The *bac* really was far away now. Too exhausted to cry, overwhelmed by shame and powerlessness, I stayed at home, praying to all the gods of survival on the planet, while Mother went off on a steel stretcher to have her head and stomach pumped in the town's hospital.

This drama hammered home just how useless my existence was. So there was nothing to live for, not even my sweet little face and curly hair? I was nothing but a burden? From that point, what makes you carry on is not really any form of desire, but more a basic instinct for life in its humblest sense. The same instinct that lives in farmed animals, which, although mutilated, force-fed and tortured, fuss about at the feet of their abuser because he is all they know and they only eat thanks to him.

On her return, Mother was in tatters. It was as if she was gradually losing her mind. I witnessed her become completely untethered, plunging into an abyss of confusion and eccentricities at the expense of everyone around her – child, friends, neighbours. The postman was one of those to suffer. Overnight, this nameless civil servant with no history and no apparent rancour, who worked tirelessly to transport those sometimes happy, sometimes sombre bureaucratic fragments of our lives, became a bird of ill omen. Sensing some nameless doom, Mother stopped saying hello to him.

'This fellow is jinxed!' she shouted one morning as he went past.

I wasn't sure how serious being jinxed was, but I sensed there was a high risk of contagion nonetheless, so I decided to keep my distance too. At the end of his round, when he dropped off our post sometime around midday, he seemed to me to be sweating, his eyes dull, his face marked with terrible fatigue. He'd drop off our letters and head away at top speed, his puny body hunched over on his steel bicycle or a small motorcycle. Perhaps he had missed his treatment time … perhaps his remaining days were numbered. Shortly after he'd gone, Mother left the veranda and went to open the letterbox indignantly.

'There's no doubt about it!' she shouted. 'He really is jinxed, that fool! He should be shot!'

Was his ailment so serious that the only remedy was violent euthanasia – and with a gun at that? My agitation increased tenfold.

What plague was eating away at him? Mother's simple suspicion had transformed into condemnation, pure and simple. We needed to rid ourselves of this man and his bad luck. Curiously, the more the bills piled up in our letterbox, the more my Mother's desire to shoot him dead increased. She sent a long, anonymous letter to the postal service's head office in which she revealed everything – the symptoms, their after-effects, the bills that we hardly ever received before. It ended with a demand that the guilty party be replaced with an employee who was not contaminated.

There was no change of postman. The letter's author became increasingly inflamed. One lunchtime, when the sickly civil servant arrived, Mother waved her fists and, invoking his legendary jinx, threatened to kill him with her own hands if he didn't stop bringing his infected letters. She chased him away, hissing curses and flinging stones. Their recipient understood nothing of the spell that had been cast on him, but after this event, half of our post no longer arrived at the correct address. Mother missed the previous postman – a saintly man who carried only world peace in his bag – while reviling the current one and his dirty, infected air. It was only several months later, at the end of a medical appointment, that I dared to ask our doctor gravely how a jinx could be cured. He opened his disproportionately large mouth and, presenting two endless rows of rotten yellow teeth, gave a sonorous snort – which I rightly identified as a spontaneous, uncontrollable chuckle.

'Who's suffering from a jinx?' he asked with a splutter.

'Our postman, Sir.'

'And have you identified any symptoms?'

'Well, he's very often sweaty, he's lost a bit of weight and …'

'Well?'

'Well, Mother says that it's also because of his jinx that he only brings us bills.'

The doctor's face convulsed as he roared with laughter. What had I said that was so funny? The old man made me sit down on one of the armchairs scattered around his office and, drying his cheeks of tears, explained in detail what a jinx was. It was a far cry from the pandemic I'd feared, but the light of the truth was colder than the shadow of the imminent death I'd been afraid of. I didn't have the courage to tell him, but I understood then that, rather than just accepting it, Mother was projecting our own emptiness and bad luck onto this perfectly healthy postman.

Sometimes it was the postman, sometimes it was the bailiff (who only ever came to our house), and sometimes it was the cashier (who managed to ensure that our credit card was never accepted). That afternoon after his shift had finished, our family doctor – perhaps feeling some contrition – drove me back as far as our letter box. As soon as I opened it, an avalanche of formal notices fell at my feet.

But that wasn't the worst of it. At the age of forty, with her deep wrinkles and garland of white hair, my mother was already old. She started to forget things. She couldn't remember the word for something, then two would escape her, and I had to supply them for her. Finally came the absurdities and misinterpretations. I didn't properly understand it until later, but the treachery of her own body, exhausted by its perpetual toing and froing in the pits of existence, had turned Mother into a woman full of hatred, acrimony and jealousy. As for me, my body had changed too. How can you cope when you want – above all else – to be as flat as a plaice but are as humpy as a camel and as hairy as a yeti? But my mother didn't see it that way. What she regretted was my new sensuality – and the sighs it provoked from elderly gentlemen, the attention from horny young men, and the hatred of girls my own age. So on evenings when her self-control and affection fell away, furious from drink and emboldened by the liquor of jealousy, she would throw herself on me. She'd beat me with her belt, hit me with her fists, kick me and slap me until she was too exhausted to continue. Never with no reason – even if it was something laughably trivial. A broken glass, five minutes' delay, a dirty plate. I am Vallès.[25] Ashamed of my adolescent faults, of my unworthy self before such a good mother, I accept each blow as a blessing. I am beaten up and I applaud. Throw me around, flog me, knock me senseless – it will make me better! Hit me again – broken ribs guarantee virtue! I wake up the next morning, my skin inflamed, my face swollen, and, taking my bucket, I start to wipe up the pools of vomit, to clean the disgusting toilet, to change the soiled sheets. Then, overcome by fatigue, I collapse at the foot of the bed on which Mum is lying. I am scared of just one thing. Of losing the torturer who thinks of me only as the error of her youth.

'You aren't small anymore!' she said one day. 'From now on, call me "aunt" instead of "mum". That's quite enough.'

Yes, that umpteenth avowal of disenchantment, disgust, detestation was enough, even for me. I swore to myself that I'd find some other world and take myself off there for good. I would run

---

25   Jules Vallès (1832-1885) was a French writer and left-wing journalist who played an important role in the Paris Commune of 1871. He wrote an autobiographical trilogy, composed of *L'Enfant* (*The Child*), *Le Bachelier* (*The Graduate*), and *L'Insurgé* (*The Insurgent*). In *L'Enfant*, Vallès writes about his difficult childhood and dedicates his book to 'all those who died of boredom at school or were made to cry in the family, who, during their childhood, were tyrannised by their teachers or scolded by their parents'. [Translators' note.]

away. It wasn't the excitement of the unknown that attracted me; it was a simple survival instinct, the 'Be brave! Let's flee!' of someone who refuses to end up with their head smashed in with a rock or strangled with a coarse rope. So I ran away. I ran away because I didn't know about *zamal*, THP and coke. I didn't know that I could blast my brain, get high and be free; that I could sweat rivers and burst all the veins in my nose to get my kicks.

––––––––––

At that time, people ran away for all kinds of reasons. You were refused the last yo-yo, the badge of your dreams, the Citroën Dyane 6 of all your fantasies and it was all over! You teleported yourself with great fanfare to the other side of the planet: to Caracas, Iceland, Luang Prabang, the island of Komodo. How television stimulates the imagination! To tell the truth, you barely made it past the Z'éclair bus terminus, but your absence for two or three days was enough to get all your relatives going.

The radio announced your disappearance in such an alarming tone – it sounded like a combination of an advertisement and a death notice – that even you were scared that something had happened to you. The paper devoted a short story to it, including the very worst photograph of you. The journalist described the clothes you were wearing – you hadn't worn them for six months; that must have been the last time your parents looked at you. Finally, in a closing paragraph punctuated with spelling mistakes, you were ordered to return at once to receive the thrashing you deserved.

But in the schoolyard, you were unanimously considered a hero, the Thelma of the Car Jaune bus network, seated in the back row like the real layabouts, a piece of chewing gum between your molars, another freshly stuck under the seat. That little blob is destined to accompany you throughout your journey, because, Thelma or not, you still haven't understood that chewing gum doesn't stick to the polyester/wool seat covers on the bus – they spit it back out onto the floor where you step on it in one of your ballet pumps and it attaches to your sole.

The police barely bother looking for you. Your parents make more of an effort, your friends do less and less. Then, out of fear of the former and nostalgia for the latter, you end up going back. You time your return for the end of the afternoon so that you won't have to go to school that day. The forests are so immense, the caves are so dark, the mosquitoes are so voracious. And at this time of year, outside it is very cold at night. But you don't know about any of that. You've spent your days going round the shops in Saint-Paul. And in Saint-Pierre (everyone is always saying that the clothes there are nicer). The only viper you have come across is that cashier who gave you away to the guard at the shopping centre – all for two lousy oranges and that must-have CD of the best Réunionnais slow dances. That evening, at the home of your thirty-year-old boyfriend, who – despite all evidence to the contrary – wants you to believe he's only eighteen, you'll forget it all over a good tub of *sauté de mines* noodles. So he's a little older than you? So what? He says that love knows no age. 'Let the young girls come to me!' – he read that in a gospel somewhere.

In short, running away is the epitome of happiness.

So I ran away too. Not like a thief in the night though. When I went that day, I left a note: an explanation using terms that might be described as brief or abrupt. Not due to literary laziness, casualness or a rush to finish as quickly as possible, but because brevity was in the bones of the Dessaintes. '*I hate you, ~~mum~~ aunt. Unicorns are not carnivores. Nor alcoholics like you. Goodbye forever!*'

It was on this note that I fled Saint-Benoît, with a small suitcase barely big enough for my clothes, a French-Latin dictionary and a few comics, never to return. My actions were prompted in some part by shame and in some part by impudence, but above all I was inspired by a hereditary penchant for wreaking havoc.

---

It was a southern winter afternoon – yet another. The sky, as if to surprise me, had a paler tint than normal. In the distance, the cloud-covered peaks and the vast sugar cane plantations limited my horizons. Where to go? What to do?

On the estate, the news that I had run away prompted very little reaction. After all, I was the sixth that week. Nobody attached any importance to this umpteenth, slightly silly desire to explore. That's how adolescents are when they tire of ordinary things. They always begin to dream of pastures new, of a more carefree existence, of a brighter, mist-free future. She'll end up coming back and dying here, like the rest of us. Pah! Just wait! She'll be back. You'll see. In two weeks, she'll have come crawling back and will be begging us to forget this ever happened. She'll come to heel, like all the others! As a result they thought it best not to bother filing a missing persons report with the police. Meanwhile, I was certain that I was breaking my 'aunt's' heart. I imagined her down on her knees with remorse, awkward as a praying mantis, and I laughed at the thought. My running-away took on an air of revenge. It appeared now as a cunning response to hatred. I expected Mother to be dumbfounded, to weep waterfalls or, better still, to faint away entirely. But nay! All I was afforded was a simple, passive, almost affable '*Bé lé bon*' – 'Very well'. Nothing more. There was no bitter irony in her tone, not even a hint of surprise. '*Bé lé bon*' and that was all. No kiss goodbye, no tears and no embrace. Only the usual jumble of hatred and pride.

For desperate cases like mine, no amount of window shopping could satisfy my soul. But there was a place that did offer some salvation. A cirque. A real cirque. Not the knock-off Cirque du Soleil on rue Descartes. Not Cilaos – too spectacular, too many bends, too many tunnels! Not Mafate – too far, too many stairs, too much silence, too perfect. What remained was Salazie. Salazie: Mother's favourite cirque (making it the ultimate insult); an ochre and green ocean of rugged peaks, streams of blue water snaking between grassy domes, the site of our picnics on those rare days that had no more than five disputes; a long wall of chayote leaves, the favourite food of good old Ratus. It was a refiguration of ancient Eden where silence met the swarming forest. Is that what I was thinking? Not a bit of it. Salazie's major advantage? It was served by the bus, twice a day. For me, Salazie cost only eighteen francs from Saint-Benoît, and I could hole up with an old aunt there (one sufficiently irresponsible and riddled with Alzheimer's to welcome me in secret and believe every morning that I arrived the evening before – even when I'd already been there three weeks). However, that didn't take away from this masterpiece of nature, scented with green moss and the freezing fog of autumn, pierced with waterfalls, fringed with red paths shaded by giant ferns, bedecked with lichen and buds with barbarous shapes. But to be honest, I think I actually prefer *Mickey Parade* comics; nature bores me more than I might have imagined. I remember arriving in Salazie. There was one of those clear skies overhead, as gentle as a caress – it was like a good omen, but I was suffering too much to appreciate it. From then on, every separation was a terrible abandonment.

In Salazie, an hour feels like a day. An endlessly slow procession of yawns, torpor and boredom. As useless as a day at university – or so I presume. I suppose it could have been worse. But God in Heaven, make sure that depressed or suicidal people never go to Salazie! It could prove fatal. In Saint-Benoît, finding a three-month-old magazine is an admirable feat; in Salazie, the latest issues are a year old if you're lucky. And you might not get anything to read at all. To pass the time, people hang around in allotments growing cress, they sort leafy greens, play dominoes or cry in front of the late-afternoon telenovelas. Afterwards, they watch the comings and goings – that's to say the empty streets – while drinking a beer or chewing on a twig, leaning against a wall that is aslant. I do all of this in the first month. In the second, I throw myself frenziedly into planting chayotes. In the third, I fish for tilapia in the Mare à Poule d'Eau, where I notice there are very few moorhens – or *poules d'eau* as we call them. In the fourth, I'm taking antidepressants to combat my acute ennui. At eighteen, I'm a little young for all this. Let's just say that the Dessaintes are precocious in every respect.

But I survive despite it all because, twelve kilometres from Salazie, there is a cinema. All the young people, including me, go there once a fortnight. We're not film buffs. It's more for the want of anything better to do. But there too we face a terrible problem: the ticket office is ruled with an iron fist by a man called Lil Leg. The customers suffer from no illusion: behind this pleasant nickname lies one of the thickest brutes in all France's overseas dominions – perhaps even beyond. Though Lil Leg has one leg a good sight shorter than the other, he makes up for it with a big personality and an exceedingly long arm. Lil Leg wakes in a fury, breakfasts in a rage and then takes himself off to the cinema to grumble at his two colleagues. When he goes on duty for the Saturday evening showing, he is always in a foul mood. The auditorium is already full, resounding with jokes and good humour. People shout out to one another from one row to the next, their feet casually resting on unoccupied seats. The red of the chairs and the lipstick, the velvet auditorium, the garnet carpet: it all makes us forget the horrible frog green of Salazie. For a few hours you believe happiness is possible. A kiss here, an old lady nearly falls over there. Everyone laughs. At the back, in the shadow of the projection room, there's a bit of courting going on. But this is all before the curtain rises. Before the arrival of Lil Leg. A bit bent under the weight of the years, but with a sense of majesty nonetheless, Lil Leg enters. Even the seats tremble as people stand to attention. 'What's that? There's no space left?' He separates couples, parents from their children, girls from their friends. He gives the best seat to someone barely able to find one, relegates those who laugh too loudly to the back rows and threatens anyone who frowns with his fists. 'You, there! Get to the back!' He's obeyed immediately. 'What! Say that again! Did I hear you right?' Nobody dares to speak. Lil Leg instantaneously transforms the chaos into the tranquillity of a graveyard. On our best behaviour, we watch the film and then quickly head back to Salazie, praying that Lil Leg never comes to live there.

---

However much I deliberated, tossing and turning in the midst of an active assembly of bedbugs, it was impossible to find anything truly fulfilling in Salazie. 'What are you going to do now?' the busy vermin in the mattress seemed to ask. It was time to attend to the most urgent issue and work with good grace. Isolated from the type of patronage that can support a brilliant destiny, knowing only Latin, Greek and history, and having a literary *bac* as my sole qualification, I had just two choices: sell bunches of cress at the entrance to Hell-Bourg or sell chayotes by a bend in the road at the weekend. In short, I had every chance of joining the sixty percent of young people living on the island who were unemployed. It's a way of life like any other, after all. The fertile soil of a vegetable garden, a few aubergine plants, a little wander along the silty paths, preceded by an ownerless dog. That's all there was to do. And there I remained, on the edge of the world, for one year, then two.

During these two years of deliberate amnesia, the Dessaintes continued their life down on the coast. A little disjointed, a little chaotic. In other words, the same as usual. I didn't know how many of them there were. Or what had become of them. To tell the truth, after my father left, most of the Dessaintes had paid us one or two visits and then, like him, had kept a good distance from our misfortune. Each to their own, everyone to the *dévinèr*.

―――――――――

We never suspect the tricks fate is playing on us behind our backs. Reason buckles under the iron rod of hope and madness, and we always believe the entire world is happy except for us. Absurdly, we imagine everyone else lives in a peaceful snow-globe world, in a confetti of good fortune. But once you start listening to other people, you realize that the world has changed for them as well and has unleashed torrents of tears and wonders, unbeknown to you.

Well before the night Father disappeared, madness had joined destitution in the lives of the other Dessaintes. Criminality had spread from one member of the family to another, suffocating what remained of their conscience and, eventually, flinging them into a corner of a dark cell. The lives of entire families had been turned upside down. What else was to be expected? What redemption was ever possible?

Increasingly underhand, moving faster than they did before, the Dessaintes then tried their hand at theft. A few threatened people with a knife, while others raped, but they were scared of strangers so they always tried it out on a sister, a younger brother or a sickly cousin first. And that was just the start. The Dessaintes had eaten too much mud: they were mad.

They were all anyone spoke about in the working-class neighbourhoods on the east of the island. Rigged cockfights and the Dessaintes. The Dessaintes flying into a rage. The Dessaintes stealing all of the wasps' nests. The Dessaintes listening to music too loudly. A mayor is looking to hire a few henchmen. He takes on half a dozen Dessaintes. You can't find your bichon frise. The Dessaintes are using some funny bait for their shark fishing! A carpenter is missing some lumber. The Dessaintes have a new pergola. Your daughter is pregnant. One of the Dessaintes men has disappeared. You're missing five pigeons. The Dessaintes are building an aviary.

One morning, under the banyan tree where the men of Beaufonds met to play poker, someone opened a newspaper while waiting for four latecomers. Only to find a picture of their corpses crammed into the corner of page three, between some sensationalist article and a car on fire. The day before, these arrogant lads had had the cheek to call two of the Dessaintes sons of bitches! Astonishment. It was too much. Tongues loosened between the clicks of dominoes – they couldn't play cards as they were a few players down. That tribe of filth and incest had really done it now; they'd tipped the island's ratty scales too far this time. The surviving Beaufonds boys – that bunch with nothing to do, always on the lookout for the latest drama – called the police. Anonymously, of course. But certain of one thing: those nutcases, the Dessaintes, were guilty.

To the callers' great disappointment, the police refused to come, though two female social workers were dispatched a few days later. They arrived one morning, neither smiling nor frowning, and planted themselves in front of the bar as if it were a rostrum. Before the incredulous crowd (who were as highly strung as an orchestra on the day of a concert) they advocated constraint, denounced scandal and failings in education, and preached the benefits of a rapid reintroduction of the death penalty or, failing that, a widespread rollout of vasectomies. Faced with silence from their audience, the eldest civil servant ordered immediate financial supervision here and there, separated a few parents from their children and then asked to be taken to a sink. Then she washed her hands right up to her shoulders in plenty of water and, her conscience clear, left without saying goodbye. She was hardly out the door before the news spread throughout the neighbourhood: 'A female social worker has been killed by a machete in the garden of those scoundrels, the Dessaintes. A second is at death's door.' It was thus, in the space of two years, that the mentally disturbed Dessaintes became murderers.

The mayors called the police themselves. They were tired of paying these mercenary henchmen; their bloody exploits were now making them very unpopular. This time, two magistrates, five journalists and twenty-three policemen were mobilized and, one after the other, broke down the front doors of all the houses where the Dessaintes lived. The police officers turned up in helmets, prowled suspiciously through the rooms, carted off a few suspects and placed a notice in the sitting room obliging the others to appear in court. All the male Dessaintes were indicted and then tried: the luckiest at the magistrates' court, the less salubrious ones at the court of assizes. The trials began the following week in jam-packed courtrooms in the neighbourhoods of Champ-Fleuri and rue Juliette-Dodu.

Hundreds of neighbours made the trip to Saint-Denis, all eager to acquire a few more sordid details about the lives of the Dessaintes. The defendants arrived in court unshaven and with their heads bowed, wearing handcuffs and slippers, and told the presiding judge what had brought them there. Sitting in Salazie in front of a few press cuttings and a television playing the news on a loop, I followed this great flood of the Dessaintes' achievements. This was how I learned that I had an uncle who was a pimp and another who was a thief, while a third sold *zamal* to children from nice neighbourhoods. And this was the best of them. But what a surprise: three uncles! And cousins by the dozen! All ferocious fellows! True Dessaintes: drunkards, fighters, respected right across the island despite never having read a single fable by La Fontaine! As for local poets, let's not even go there.

For weeks, La Réunion was gripped by the case. In Saint-Benoît, Mother could no longer show her face; every time she stepped outside, this newfound notoriety brought a torrent of abuse down upon her. Then a new family stole the limelight: fifteen murders in six months. We were no match for these guys from the town of Le Port, and the judge wanted to expedite the first case to devote himself to the second. On the day of the verdict, the Dessaintes managed to call on unknown reserves of energy; they prepared a vigorous and belligerent defence. In a single, unanimous voice they justified their moribund existence – if they were guilty, the world was hardly innocent!

One of them, the least mad, made his way to the witness box but, after cracking all his fingers, made a dismal display; he suddenly chickened out and ran off to sit back down again. A second replaced him. No luck! He couldn't remember a single word of the long-winded speech they'd laboured over. Happily, a third came to the rescue. He uttered a plea that his co-defendants thought wasn't so bad, considering he'd pinched the lines a minute before from a court-appointed lawyer dozing close by:

'There has always been a glass dome between the heads of the Dessaintes and the sky that maintained the illusion that the stars were both beautiful and well within reach. That ambition and a decent job you could work at everyday were enough. That it was enough to be honest, fair and good. But in time, I learnt that this was all a cheap trick, a fabrication intended to preserve the peace of the wealthy, to avoid mass slaughter – to ensure that hope remains. What could be more dangerous than a man without hope, a man who has seen all his illusions shattered? Ten years of battle for us *Cafres*, ten years of struggle: that definitely equals ten years of peace somewhere else. Ten years of being too busy with self-improvement to think about revolution. The first Dessaintes certainly tried to make it through. The later generations too. Clumsily perhaps; in vain certainly. They failed to succeed because the people who had installed this glass dome – let's call it a curse, misfortune, bad luck, universal lies – were the only ones who could take it away. So we had to write our own laws, erect our own little boundaries, forge truths from the lies fed to us. Our methods may follow a different logic but they were the only way we had to advance ourselves a little. Or to try at any rate.

'The Dessaintes aren't bad people. Just people without hope, whose ineffectual obduracy, many faults and repeated failures ended up taking on an air of fantasy. They hung on in there longer than anyone else. They refused to relinquish the wand of optimism. But all for nothing. Effort but no reward, pain but no gain. Just scum tossed about by the thunderous ocean. And so eventually they let go, and out of their depth they sank down. Down to the depths. Deeper and deeper. After three centuries of effort, they gave in. They found themselves at that border where morality meets depravity. Destined, as it was written, "To accomplish nothing and die overworked."'

Overworked is what the judge was! Inured to these tall tales worthy of the Wild West, he wiped his glasses five times, jangled his office keys, issued a bored yawn and adjourned the case. All these trials, he thought, how homogenous they were! One wondered if all the defendants on earth didn't belong to the same enormous family of cretins! The hearing was suspended. In the deliberation room, between coffees, the magistrates fretted about whether they'd have to work late or not.

The trial resumed. The prosecutor put on a performance as usual. He raised his arms to the heavens, as if he had a hernia in his armpits. He wagged his head from right to left, squinted for no reason and finally fixed his eyes on the packed courtroom. The crowd was getting impatient.

'Is the old cock going to lay an egg, or what? The theatre is on the other side of the courtyard. He looks like a sea lion in a dressing gown!'

This last comment sparked a huge peal of laughter in the courtroom. It felt like the first day of the sales, the start of a new school year. Eventually the gallery was cleared, and two guards were placed at each entrance to shoot warning glances at all those gluing their faces to the window panes in the door. 'This has gone on long enough!' roared the presiding judge. And on that note, the small group of defendants were sent to the detention centre in Le Port for the rest of their lives. And that is how most of the Dessaintes disappeared without ever having run away.

From then on, they could be seen behind the high steel fences of a Bastille-like death camp, contemplating the mountains and the sun. The first winter arrived not long after they had been admitted. With stealthy, quiet steps, it crept up the paths of the prison garden, draping every petal with an arid veil, draining each stem of its rich sap, withering the juicy fruit and shrivelling the unruly vines. By the time the Dessaintes realized that the few buds around them were turning brown, summer had flown to the other side of the world, taking with it all their early hopes: a miraculous escape by helicopter, the unexpected dismissal of the charge, immediate rehabilitation. These wishes had withered like the frangipani trees. All that remained was a soft and bitter exhalation in the cold of the night.

And then, one foggy morning, everything had gone. The dragonfly with the Persian tail. The expectation of a visit, the comfort of a familiar face full of empathy. All of these things were entombed in an eternal winter of stone and oblivion. So they went back to doing what they did best. Lashing out. At doors, faces, guards, chaplains, psychiatrists. In a desperate measure, the most violent were sent to plant cabbages in the vegetable garden of the Rémire-Montjoly prison in French Guiana. The others were treated with tear gas and solitary confinement. And then, one day, one of them blurted out a revelation: 'It's not so bad here!'

Another winter was in full swing in the southern hemisphere. The third since their arrest. What seemed like a century in Salazie. Their passionate impulses had faded, and with them the ferocious orgies of the first few weeks – the caresses of men with the hearts of beasts, the habitual rutting episodes in the latrines. All these antics now just seemed like a pointless way to relieve boredom. Only once a year did they indulge themselves, succumbing to sudden salacious fever that tormented their flesh. Then, as one, the horde would sweep over a newcomer, envying the pungent scent of freedom, their obvious innocence. But although they threw themselves at these new orifices, they no longer had the appetite for it; they were like old men with enfeebled imaginations. They tottered in, shot their load with great difficulty and left in disgust, yammering: 'My perineum! My perineum! My perineum hurts so much!'

Time and remorse, combined with vigorous clouts from the most zealous guards, had ground down their wild urges, their rages of yesteryear. On either side of the world, the Dessaintes began to visit the prison chaplains. They came in peace this time. Some converted to Islam, others discovered they were Protestants, and one returned to the Judaism of an ancestor that only he seemed to know about. In short, for want of forgiveness, they all set out in search of the sacred. In the midst of former paedophiles, precocious burglars and unrepentant murderers, they began to live happily, their conscience at peace. Abstinent men in an omniscient panopticon, for the first time they felt they were no longer being left to fend for themselves. They learned to read; they became better at everything – better at planting leafy greens, better at playing football, better at poetry, better at drawing. And finally, they became better prisoners. They requested books, attended classes at the prison school, prepared for the Grand Raid race[26], sat the *brevet*. They put the same serious application and ardour into their work as scholars and sportsmen as they had once put into beheading old ladies, robbing little boys, hanging dogs alive and disembowelling pregnant cats.

Sometimes they would gaze towards the free world and be engulfed in a great wave of sadness. But they'd soon come to their senses. They still had decades left to serve, and it was for the best. If they were released, the very next day they'd massacre one of their own, assault a little girl and saturate the local press with news of their parricides. All the Dessaintes knew it. In the eyes of the normal world, spinning in its normal way, they would always be no more than a gang of pariahs, and pariahs only do what is expected of them. Were they to renounce a life of crime and try to lead an orderly life, the world would accuse them of just pretending to be good, of faux humility and utter hypocrisy. Were they to kill again, in the very year of their release, the world would be outraged at these wolves in sheep's clothing, whom it had greeted with patience and optimism, had welcomed with open arms. This much they had sensed: the world would only be on the lookout for their

---

26  The Grand Raid, also known as *La Diagonale des Fous*, is a 164 km race with 10,000 metres of ascent that generates incredible fascination among locals. Highly recommended if seeking blisters and aches.

next moment of weakness. The world would blame them for not changing, while refusing to see that they had. All that was expected of them was bad news and explosions of fury. Their desire for peace and harmony, for a small house in La Plaine-des-Palmistes, for a view of the sea: none of these would be accepted. So they preferred to stay put. That's the way it is and that's that!

Outside, time passed, and nobody thought of paying them a visit. Everyone considered it best to start a new life of their own, away from each other. Mothers and children reinvented their lives, outside of crime. The Dessaintes became small clans – the free, those in prison, the ones in custody, the exiled, the dead. Parallel worlds, revolving in total ignorance of each other, like planets without a sun.

Rumour had it that the Dessaintes who were free – those who were still alive – had migrated to the northern countries, far enough at least to ensure that news from the island no longer reached them. Rumour also had it that as soon as they had landed on those cold and distant shores, the prevailing Puritan morality had provided them with a new worldview, coating a thin layer of shame over the inveterate hedonism of their pasts. With plenty of bad neighbourhoods and cheap liquor at hand, their metamorphosis wasn't going to be easy. But apparently they put so much of their formerly epicurean hearts into it that, after an austere year or so of self-denial, they all ended up marrying for love and throwing their former instincts for debauchery over the ramparts of oblivion. Thanks to the distance they put between them and their former lives, the children and then the grandchildren were successfully exorcized. This branch of the family was saved. Was Father among them? I never found out.

———————

Three years passed. Three years of nothing much. From time to time, I left Salazie to go to Saint-André, or Saint-Denis, or more rarely Saint-Paul. But never to Saint-Benoît. It's almost as if the smaller the island is, the more sedentary you become – like Bouchot mussels.

I regularly accompanied my aunt to the Sainte-Marie cemetery. In all honesty, to call it a cemetery wouldn't be quite right, since the graves were nothing but big rectangles of flowers from which – with great difficulty – a name, a date or a Creole inscription emerged, reminding us that each bouquet of hydrangeas, busy lizzies or roses had taken root in the heart of a man.

What a number of young Dessaintes had already lived and died! And what lives they had lived! Unlike anyone else's. Lives worth nothing at all. In one of the most remote corners of memory's vast pasture, facing the foamy sea, their tombstones leaned sadly, their epitaphs bleached by the sun, the weather and oblivion. Here lay Lila, who died of thrombosis and of a melancholic *je-ne-sais-quoi*. There, behind a thorn bush, another grave with a cruel crack in it recorded the death of two uncles devoured by the sea. Nearby lay their brother, found hanged one Whitsun evening after being labelled a descendant of slaves with unnatural tendencies. In a long letter, still smelling of the popular Ploum Ploum perfume, he had readily confessed to both, but he was under no illusions about his fellow men and their sly nature. Faced with constant harassment and eternal kowtowing to his enemies, he chose the rope, which had the merit of being silent, entirely secular and uncompromising. Not far away lay an aunt who had been strangled out of love – and no doubt a touch of annoyance – one Friday evening when she had made the mistake of asking for the TV remote and a divorce. A small group of young Dessaintes had been buried next to her – drunk and therefore happy. They had snuffed it in a car smash, their thick blood spraying across the nearby walls before flowing unhurriedly into the city's sewers. One had survived, but half-mad and reeking of petrol and bloody spittle, he had run towards the flaming bonnet as if it was an ambulance come to save him. He burnt to a crisp, screaming his head off. Armed with buckets and tarpaulins, the locals had rushed to the scene, more to drown out his unbearable screams than the flames themselves, but it was already too late. His life had dissolved into a grotesque pool of blood and mud. The mayor had donated a family crypt, and a priest – although the Dessaintes no longer believed in anything at that point – had come to solemnly bless the remaining shreds of flesh and bones. They smelt like old fish stock. This was followed by an oration punctuated by Latin phrases, Gospel sayings and enthusiastic amens. Once the bodies had been buried, the cemetery caretaker planted a few ixoras and a bed of lemongrass on the graves.

That marked the end of the Dessaintes. They had died as they had lived. For nothing! And the decline initiated in the seventeenth century had calmly completed its levelling work where it had all begun: by the sea.

_____

From the cemetery, it was a short distance to the bus stop serving Saint-Benoît. Once in town, all you had to do was walk past the small semi-detached houses of Cité Poivre – a few cube-shaped houses and an old building that Father used to say was guarded by a sphinx with a goat's head and a squirrel's paws – and you'd come to the main road that led almost directly to rue Descartes, since it was rumoured that the Dessaintes were back in their old house. This was surely for the best after their exploits in the Beaufonds neighbourhood. No news from Mother for three years. You might not miss her, but you're curious. One day, I felt a terrible urge to go back there, just to see her, maybe even throw a few insults in her face, like the bad Dessaintes that I was.

The evening before my return to Saint-Benoît was long, pensive and upsetting. I couldn't sleep and paced up and down. There was no doubt that nothing good would come of this reunion; I could already foresee arguments of all kinds, tears every day, a litany of invectives, repeated skirmishes, profound depression, loud shameful retorts and the futile regret that followed. And anything unreasonable and petty was put to use straight away in the Dessaintes household. Mother, unbridled with rage, would surely call at every gate in rue Descartes to denounce both my desertion and my pointless return, cursing my inconstancy and ingratitude in front of every neighbour who opened their door. Having lost her head entirely, she would ruin my reputation once and for all. After all, in the Dessaintes household, dirty laundry was never aired at home but only in public.

It would be a cold reunion.

Outside, the first rays of sunshine could already be seen. I looked out at the world, which was still dusted with sleep, and, like a tired old mare that has tasted freedom and now rears up at the memory of the stall and the blinkers, I began to stamp my foot. What now?! I still had to silently swallow the traditional catechism:

that the Dessaintes were nothing, had nothing, achieved nothing? If only I had a more persuasive counter-argument than long, drawn-out sighs! My paltry successes in Salazie would perfectly justify my mother's criticism. The time had come to be held to account and, objectively speaking, apart from the money I made growing chayotes and various types of leafy greens, my bottom line wasn't great.

———————

Nothing had really changed in our neighbourhood. Everywhere, there were the same terraces adorned with *lambrequins*,[27] the same fences garlanded with bright-red crotons, the same leaky tin roofs that let in both the sun and the rain. But time had added to the scene, embroidering a lacework of rust and mould on top of it all. Cyclones, poverty and the total lack of any conscientious local tradesmen made the houses look like they were haunted.

After a few minutes' walk, I caught sight of the large louvres that I knew so well. I had reached the key artefact of this living museum: our old house in rue Descartes. And, in the courtyard, the orange tree from my childhood! The demon of yesteryear had survived! Planted in the middle of the ruined garden between the river and the road, scarred by the years and the rain, it too had clung to life. Laden with early fruit, and a full thirteen years after the terror it had inflicted on me, something like a smile and a plea for peace bloomed in its stunted branches. 'Peace? Never! Bring me a sword!'

———

27  A wooden or metal decorative frieze that hangs down from the roof of a traditional Reunionese/Creole house and hides the gutters.

I shouted at the top of my voice to anyone who cared to listen.

Talking of swords … What the Dessaintes call a sword bears no resemblance to what the Samurai would call a sword. It's no more than a thug's machete. But here, in this topsy-turvy tropic where everyone walks on their hands, people have mastered the art of taking one name to refer to something else. The island chameleon is actually a lizard, sweets are biscuits, pastilles are sweets, pistachios are peanuts, and Arabs, also known as 'Z'arabes', come from India. As could be expected with all this confusion, someone brought a glass of water instead. They led me to a corner of the garden where I found a lady somewhat marked by age. She was a little deaf, and seemed lonely and contemplative – like all those old people bearing their wrinkles and their pain who are left alone as long as they keep quiet. It was Mum. She was in a wheelchair now. 'That's what you deserve!' I thought.

And what did we do, Mother and I? We argued. We started straight away and continued for the whole time that we spent together. In the mornings, on days when the weather was bad, during sleepless nights. We argued about what we'd done during the years we were apart, we argued about everything we had had to do to keep from dying, we argued about how we'd had enough of arguing. Why would we jump into each other's arms? We never knew how to do that. But the middle finger salute and a couple of kicks to her wheelchair, and all was forgiven. Hurling insults in the hope of still being loved, throwing presents out the window when you want them more than anything, begging the other to leave when leave means stay: whose fault is it if we lack common sense and simple logic? Showing your true, dirty colours, exposing your misery and still expecting to be forgiven the way you'd forgive a child. Convinced that you'll learn to behave just as soon as someone accepts your disgusting manners and your debased condition, as soon as someone contemplates you tenderly, loves you unconditionally. Alas, no one ever will. There's an empty ocean full of broken promises. You are naked and alone, a hopeless case. Surrounded by two hundred and forty billion exoplanets, seven billion people and as many temptations, you have no right to anything. Love you? Forgive you? Try to understand you? Never! Real forgiveness can only count to two. After that, people ignore you, shun you, despise you, hate you and curse you. With good reason. Contemplate the void and throw yourself into it now! Nobody knows you anymore.

---

In between fights, I wrote. The eternal obsession. The only thing. Not a day passed without a scribble. Because I have no talent in any other area. Because we search in the darkness. Because we know nothing. Because we can never achieve what we want. Because every cold night is inhabited by writers who, faced with your cadaverous solitude, still have the decency to console you. In the company of these novelists, I end up believing I'm one of them. At the end of the day, happiness really comes down to very little: laying out everything in a book the way bodies are placed in a grave.

I write because I've finally realized my destiny, because I want to become what I am. To achieve a new dignity.

So I write books. To challenge myself, to please myself. Unhappy books, with a thousand and one lost joys, hearts laid low by loneliness – infinite sadness. What else can you write with your partisan rage? What else can you write for a mouth that has run out of words?

I readily confess, brazen as a liar: I deal only in extremes – the fatigue of fighting men, the intoxication of the thirsty. Let the mad, the antisocial, the worthless women, the quarrelsome, the stubborn, the suicidal, the hands that tremble – let them be mine! Let those that are fearless because they have nothing to lose, those forgotten by everyone, those soft faces with obstinate hearts – let them be mine! For here, their pain is told and their disgrace blessed. By night, as by day, I wanted them to exist here, to have an ode to their madness, a book that avenges them even as it absolves them. God doesn't love us anymore, but we love ourselves!

———————

There were only two Dessaintes who hadn't been locked up left in La Réunion: Mother and I. Between manuscripts, I'd had to find something to feed us and, between meals, I had to go and look for paid employment. Mother and I joined that large community of job seekers roaming the streets of the city in search of a 'small key' – an expression we use for odd jobs, often badly paid and illegal – that would close the door on our incessant troubles once and for all. But like most other job seekers on the east coast, we found nothing.

The mayor, holding his nose, ended up organizing a public works programme for us on the waterfront. Pruning vacoa trees, picking up leaves and used condoms, burning piles of dry grass, maintaining the kiosks along the Rivière des Roches, watching the fat women from Saint-Benoît try to walk themselves fit: the job itself wasn't very demanding. For the second time, we were catching a bit of a break in La Réunion.

Work started at seven in the morning among the avenues of vacoas. In groups of two or three, we'd stroll along the calm seashore, taking innumerable breaks, shooting the breeze. Occasionally we'd pull up a few weeds, but when the sun became unbearably hot it meant the morning was over. And all our afternoons were free. Everyone went back to their housing estate to idle away the time in front of their TV, look after their children and eat their *carri*. We weren't rich but we weren't unhappy either. In any case, the question of happiness was seldom on anyone's mind. You love your car and your mistress – or *tantine*, as we say. You call the radio when you lose your dog. You're a little envious of your stupid neighbour and you spend too much time in traffic. It mightn't be exactly joyful, but at least you have a quiet life; you enjoy a good-quality sound system at the weekend, an occasional picnic, a few family get-togethers, a good chicken *carri* cooked over a wood fire. Everything else is a matter of perfect indifference. Resting in the shade of the mango and lychee trees, in the dry and rainy seasons, this bedrock of nonchalance was our life too.

Wedged between the mountains and the eternal sea, we enjoyed scraping by and making the best of things, but best of all was our sublime, sun-drenched boredom. Besides having two or three children, turning on the TV, sorting out a 'small key', what else was there to do on this god-forsaken island, anyway? Life, though paved with violence and bitterness, flowed by more slowly and less chaotically, it seemed, than in faraway Europe. It was better to stay and do something here. But what?

To tell the truth, we thought about it for a year – as long as my job lasted. A few days before the official end of the contract, after having triumphantly overcome an army of Mafia-like bankers, career advisers and *déviners*, we decided to take over a run-down snack bar on the waterfront – in the very place where I did my pruning every morning. Opening a snack bar was pretty much our only option; that said, a snack bar is also a guarantee of success. In car parks, in front of a school, near a shopping centre, along the beach – you can always find one of those shacks with their enormous dodo signs,[28] partly obscured by one or two PVC tables. There are as many of them on the island as there are unemployed people.

Open from 7:30 am, standing in a rectangular patch of shade you can order anything that ordinary culinary ethics might forbid: three-sauce sandwiches; *pain bouchon, pain américain, pain dakatine, pain carri*;[29] glucose-saturated fizzy drinks of cornflower-blue, blush-pink or lemon-yellow; pale, amber and dark beers; sticky sweets. There were also the ubiquitous *barquettes*, plastic tubs filled with a thick layer of plain rice covered with beans and some kind of *carri* – chicken, pork, beef, fish or goat at best; at worst, things that are best left unsaid. They're very filling, and full of fat and salt. Every Reunionese has a personal favourite food truck, their favourite *carri*, their favourite side dish. And they eat, comfortable in the knowledge that though the world may stop spinning, snack bars will go on. They will be there for all time, at the service of hungry tummies – the ultimate refuge from hunger, thirst, anorexia, fatigue,

---

28  The dodo is a big bird incapable of flying that ambled happily around La Réunion before the Europeans wiped it out. This bird is now a symbol of the island and of the local beer bearing the same name.

29  Sandwiches *au gratin*, with peanut butter or filled with *carri*, respectively.

boredom and loneliness. In short, what we needed was a snack bar.

From then on, routinely, for several months, you could almost hear the fizzing in our skulls: the complex jumble of projects, meals, sandwiches and stocks to be prepared. Dessaintes with responsibilities! Better still, with clients! What an audacious, extravagant plunge we had taken! The previous owner had been nabbed for having served Creole appetizers called 'bouchons' filled with dog meat instead of the pork with Kaffir lime as advertised. He handed us the keys one Sunday morning with a deep sigh, before returning to his new job: a supervisory position at the animal pound. The following week, our snack bar raised its brightly coloured awning to the sky. To the kitchen, worthless women!

From morning to late afternoon, I couldn't catch my breath. Between the suppliers, the customers and the invoices, I was busy in the kitchen, toasting spices, answering the phone, and preparing the *barquettes* as soon as I'd finished the sandwiches. Mother was in charge of the till; I did everything else. Our lives became an endless procession of orders, builders and their salacious allusions, and ever-present barflies and inveterate drinkers. We started inventing new recipes, doubling *carri* portions and giving out the odd geranium-infused rum on the sly. And the customers kept coming back for more. Running a snack bar is like being a doctor. You don't just look after the stomach; you look after everything else too: heart problems, anxiety, addictions. Between ladlefuls of butter beans, we had to listen to shameless confessions, unfunny jokes and pitiful requests. No! The establishment doesn't sell Solpaks[30] on credit. Of

---

30  A triangle-shaped juice box that was very popular in La Réunion in the 1980s-1990s.

course we only accept money! To make a long story short: within two months we'd realized that our clients consisted of nothing but bulimic, diabetic, greedy scoundrels. We were very busy, but we weren't making any money. After four months I had to diversify our activities. From then on, as well as the traditional *pain bouchon gratiné* and *rougail boucané* cucumber salad, I had the good idea of selling the *zamal* that Mother and I grew behind a row of Canna lilies in our spare time.

Nobody minded. Quite the opposite! That bit of land had lain fallow for decades, demand was booming in Saint-Benoît, and our prices were astonishingly low. Even the less well off – the sick, the delinquent, the long-term unemployed – could afford to buy from us. It was democratic *zamal*, and the sea spray gave it something extra – a slightly sour tang. As Mother liked to say, morals don't pay social security contributions.

From then on, our business did much better than we had ever expected, even in our wildest dreams.

We had suffered unfairly but now success had found us, it worshipped us and protected us, because we were deserving. Or maybe it had just lighted on the wrong people.

By cleverly evading the taxman, we managed to make small, then large and finally very large profits, which we decided to invest in renting a small piece of farmland on the black market. Hemp, mallards, chickens and tenrecs lived side by side there, and a recluse from Bras-Canot, who loved nature and quadrupeds more than his own kind, looked after it for us, in exchange for twenty eggs and half a dozen organic joints a day. In this manner, the first six months passed as quickly as one. We even hired a cook in the middle of the year. In less than 18 months, all three of us had gained ten kilos. And within two years, that scumbag of a cook opened his own snack bar and disappeared, stealing half of our kitchen utensils. But we couldn't press charges because we'd stolen them ourselves – from the neighbouring school's canteen.

Despite these minor setbacks, the business was doing well, and we were even thinking of expanding: home delivery; rum punch, *sarcive* and salad evenings; vegetarian *barquettes*; all-organic sandwiches; a second snack bar at the other end of the waterfront – there were plenty of options. In just a few months, we had become the most popular snack bar in town. So despite the anonymous phone calls, threats of being hanged, furious *Bonn la moucate*[31] graffiti and decapitated black hens that welcomed us in the mornings, our clients kept multiplying like the biblical loaves – or rather like *macatias*, our own sweet Reunionese version. But above all – and this is worth stressing – we were never one of those crooks that pass off one meat as another. Sautéed pork was sautéed pork where we were concerned. No cats in our sausages. No dogs in our blood sausage. In short, we were honest. When it came to cooking at least. And wasn't that the most important thing?

---

So how did this success story veer off track? For, as you may have guessed in light of my chronic misfortune, this period of bliss was short-lived. There came a day of great heat, the last in December. Exhausted, Mother and I were shadows of ourselves as we headed into the New Year. But what could possibly scare us now?

---

31  Reunionese insult. Possible translation here: 'Son of a bitch'.

We'd left the snack bar a little late, I remember. It was exactly 7:34 pm. We passed a drunk. A drunk staggering through the languid streets of Saint-Benoît. Nothing could be more normal. He saw us, and recognized us as the last Dessaintes on this side of the world. If he'd passed by without taking aim at our belated good fortune, we'd simply have gone on our way. But he had to point his finger at us. He had to insult our contentment and call us names.

The whole street was buzzing with his abuse. What sort? The dirtiest, the most monstrous, the most humiliating that the devil has invented. The type that tears your heart asunder and sucks out your pride. This broadcast had barely been bawled out before little ones began asking their parents questions and old people started recalling who the Dessaintes really were. All it took was one spark. Just one. Is burying something the same as forgetting it? And is forgetting forgiving? They would never change, those Dessaintes. They were born scum. And whatever had happened to them, hadn't they brought it on themselves? Beware! There was only one left. Now there are two of them. How many would there be in a year's time? The whole pack would come back and spread their dirty seeds in our pure and peaceful town.

By the next day, the whole street had taken on a completely different aspect. It was vibrating with curses. We were monsters. Inbred criminals. Scoundrels born to lose. Evil, haughty, tyrannical, irascible, dishonest, violent. We were nothing, worse than nothing.

A month later, as I crossed that same street, the drunk, emboldened by his latest floozy – a waster just like him – spat in my face. Then came two slaps, soon followed by three … five … ten. I could hear him screaming. We finally got them, those scumbags. And then there was silence. Everything around me stopped abruptly.

There was a ring of bodies, a human carousel sometimes pausing, always turning. And no one to stop it. Well done him, they said. From then on, nothing could hold me back. So, yes, I put the knife to his throat and made a slow incision. What was I doing with a knife? I don't know. I'm a Dessaintes. That's the way it is and that's that.

If it hadn't been for that beastly crowd, I'd probably have slit his throat. Why stop? Let me be a scoundrel to the very end. After all, I wasn't born for any other role. What was it that I really wanted to kill? People's refusal to admit that you can be different to how they imagine you to be. They would have me lose my faith. Not in God! That impotent, autistic old man has never received a single prayer born from my distress. My faith in myself. I would no longer believe myself capable of anything. Except wallowing in lies and larceny, in fury and in filth. Why bother? Because of that faint instinct, that compelling drive for life and goodness buried beneath the mud? A leopard never changes their spots, they say, as if they're some kind of superior animal, these wolves in sheep's clothing. People never change! They're wicked beyond redemption and yet they call my crimes unspeakable. It would be easier to talk about what I have not yet done. But every day, no one tries as hard as I do. Each of my crimes is followed by even greater remorse and atonement more ferocious than the offence itself. So how will cases like mine be judged? Who's worse: those who watch people make mistakes and do nothing to stop them or those who keep hanging on, who ignore the fact they live on a precipice and keep on trying anyway?

But let's leave it there. Mother is moaning and her last days in the light are now numbered. As for me, I don't have much longer All the Dessaintes die before they've had a chance to live.

―――――――――

I found myself called before a judge from the court of assizes for having attempted to slit a man's throat, evade tax and commit every other offence they could conceive of. I didn't defend myself. I had been doing so in vain for twenty-three years. I don't feel any guilt. Perhaps I've grown up to be like the sons of a mafia boss, convinced that it's the rest of the world that has a problem. I don't possess much anymore, apart from the name Dessaintes, this D that, though it may not recall the splendour of virtue, at least retains the initial letter of our dignity.

At the end of the two-day hearing, the court reached its verdict and passed its sentence. I could have chosen another path; I had no excuse. An example had to be set. For these crimes, and for all the others, I was sent to a prison in the heart of Saint-Denis for eight years.

These days, I go back and forth to the prison library, where my fingers clutch frozen poems, the names of a hundred authors who are now my only family – my only gods. I'll most certainly die in their company. In the courtyard, which is barely bigger than a basketball court, I keep a low profile. I am among women who are much like me. After pottery lessons and other such trivial classes designed to make us believe that redemption is possible, I read in a low voice, like a bandit, like a voyeur, in dark and secret nooks. I've got a notebook, a few sheets of paper and a few pens. This will suffice as my world from now on. When I was asked if I wanted to take anything with me to prison, all I asked for were the scraps of text I'd been writing since I was a child. Over time, the words have flowed like a continuous, inexhaustible river, their long blue trail sliding across the page. My books recount the atrocities and splendour of the Dessaintes, the mystery of their Corsican moods. I write all night long: I forgot how to sleep years ago.

All day, on the other side of the prison's thick wall, I hear the hum of cars stuck in endless traffic jams. I'm like one of those cars: not moving an inch, then advancing just as far as the next traffic jam; following another slow-moving crowd that is itself going around in circles. All the Dessaintes were in this traffic jam. On a huge roundabout with no exit. From morning to night, the entire island seems congested, trapped in a history beyond its understanding – stuck in a past, in a curse that still incapacitates La Réunion to this day. It's as if the only force we have is inertia. We're running in a frozen race, a '*Diagonale*' of the paralysed.

Is that how it's going to end, then? With the same violence, the same deceit, the same injustice as at the start? Will darkness follow darkness? You now know the whole story: from the coasts of Africa to Saint-Denis. The wandering, the crimes and the distress that have snapped at our heels. And now, I can set this testimony down. Everyone will know. The Dessaintes tried. Ceaselessly. For all eternity.

And as for me, I've made up my mind: I'm escaping tomorrow. And that's that.